D1509984

A Trail of Broken Dreams

The Gold Rush Diary of Harriet Palmer

BY
BARBARA HAWORTH-ATTARD

Scholastic Canada Ltd.

Date	Item	Cost
March 10	50 lbs. black flour	2.25
	20 lbs. bacon	2.00
	1 bag dried apples	1.50
12	7 yards flannel	1.05
17	postage	.25
	4 hanks of yarn	.25
18	headache tablets	.25
	2 pairs flannel drawers	.25
19	sundries: tea, sugar, pepper,	3.00
	salt, baking soda	
24	1 oz iodine	.05
	1 bottle petroleum	.05
April 1	Balance Carried Forward	1.85
	beans	.35
	barley	.20
4	1 bushel potatoes	.50
	1 doz. eggs	.16

Upper Fort Garry,
Red River Settlement,
1862

May 15, 1862
Upper Fort Garry, Red River Settlement

We buried Mama today.

I didn't mean to write those words. How can she be dead when I see her at this table, head bent, pen in hand, filling the pages of this account book from edge to gutter as was her way? There, now I have blurred the ink with a tear. I have no time to cry. I must return to Mama's accounts. I need to know how we stand.

May 15, 1862, evening

I finally believe Mama is never coming back. I stood at the burying, not looking at Mama's coffin. Nor at the small grave beside her, where baby Robert was buried six weeks before. He lived only a few weeks. I divided my gaze between searching the flat horizon for Father and glaring at Mrs. Owen.

Reverend Mr. Corbett said his words hastily as dark clouds gathered on the horizon, and the wind swirled dust about our feet and into our faces. Dressed in their darkest clothes, the mourners looked like crows as they raised their hands again and again to protect their eyes from dust. I kept my arms still, and even welcomed the grit stinging my face. It was the first I'd felt anything since Mama died. Even before the last words were spoken over Mama, people turned and fled back to Fort Garry or their homes in the settlement. I lingered a moment, searching the prairie once again. Surely Father would know Mama was dead of childbed fever. Wouldn't he feel it and come home? But I saw nothing.

"Come along into the fort now, Harriet," Mrs. Owen called to me, but I ignored her. I am stubborn like that. It is one of my faults. Then she began petting and cooing over Luella, and putting her arm around William. I rushed to catch up to them and took each of their hands in mine and pulled them from her grip. They belong to Mama, not Mrs. Owen. They belong to *me*.

May 17, 1862

Our situation is not good. We have spent all our money and more. Mama obviously thought Father would return from the gold fields with riches. Why else would she run up a large debt at the Owens' store? I see from her figures that the bulk of money from the sale of Father's mill went to pay for our train and stage journey from Canada West to the

Red River Settlement. More went for Father's share in a cart and ox so he could set off for British Columbia and the gold fields. We ate the rest over the winter months.

It does not feel right to look at Mama's cramped figures — money matters are private affairs — but I overheard Mrs. Owen telling the ladies in the fort that we were penniless and orphaned. My brain is in a burning turmoil. I do not know what to do.

May 18, 1862

I berate myself for continuing to waste ink and paper to keep a reckoning of my days in Mama's account book, but I have no friends here and it makes me feel less lonely.

I spent the day roaming the fort and asking after work. I put up my hair like Mama did hers, so I'd look older than my twelve years, brushed dust from my skirt and forced a pleasant smile on my face. I tried the residence of the Hudson Bay Company's chief factor, and the officers' residences, to offer my services as a maid or cook's helper, but they had no use for me. I then tried the barracks, but one private laughed, saying I was too bony for work. I wanted to tell him that *bony* people work the hardest, but I didn't have the heart.

May 20, 1862

I will it to be otherwise, dear diary, but I have no way to provide for Luella or William. We were told yesterday to vacate the rooms Father had taken for us. I had to throw myself upon the mercies of Mrs. Owen. Her eyes narrowed as they ran up and down my thin frame, but lit up when she saw Luella, and her husband gave William flour bags to stack. I assured her Father would be back soon with bags of gold and would pay them handsomely for their trouble. She told me to sweep the floor of the store. She scooped up Luella and took her off upstairs to their rooms.

May 22, 1862

I heard Mr. and Mrs. Owen talking last night. They are making plans to return to Toronto next year. Mrs. Owen complained that she did not like all the openness of the land, and thinking about it, I cannot recall seeing her much outside the fort. When forced to leave, she hugs the walls and scurries back in at the first opportunity. But the worst is that I heard Mrs. Owen say that she wanted to take Luella with her! Luella reminds her of her baby girl who died some years back. Mr. Owen said he'd like to take William also, as he is a stout lad and, at ten, a good age to be a help. Then there was a silence. "What about Harriet?" Mrs. Owen finally asked. Her voice becomes hard when she talks of me.

Mr. Owen said he thought he could find me a position as a maid to people named Schubert, who own the tavern across the river. I cannot believe the Owens would leave me here, and take Luella and William! "That would be good," Mrs. Owen said. "She is just another mouth to feed and not an attractive one at that."

I hate her, but as I write this, I know part of what Mrs. Owen says to be true. If you put Luella and me side by side, you would never guess we were sisters, she with her blond curls and large blue eyes, and me with my limp brown hair and pasty face with red freckles that even a washing with a liberal dose of lemon juice would not remove, and eyes so contrary they don't know whether to be green or grey. So her words are true — but still they hurt.

I have lost Mama and a new brother. I will *not* lose Luella and William. I will think of something.

May 24, 1862

Today is the Queen's birthday. A volley of gunfire started the day and the soldiers marched on the small parade ground, then drink was taken liberally.

May 25, 1862

How I wish Father would come back. Between the pages of Mama's account book, I found the letter he sent to us from Fort Edmonton. He said he was well and would soon be at the gold fields. I remember when we got the letter, how Mama cried and cried. I thought to send a letter back to him telling him of Mama's death, but I don't know where to send it.

May 26, 1862

I overheard Mrs. Owen speaking of me to the captain's wife. "She does not grieve for her mother," Mrs. Owen said. "She's an unnatural child." I was stung to the bottom of my soul! I have not had time for grief. My thoughts are occupied with how to keep Luella and William. I hate Mrs. Owen! Mama would scold me for thinking so, but I can't help it. I hate her! Even if I have to help Mrs.

Sinclair do laundry for the soldiers, I will, if it means I can get away from that woman.

May 27, 1862

I left the fort this morning at dawn. I needed to escape and think without Mrs. Owen's voice rattling in my ears. I know that I should be grateful that she took us in — as Mrs. Owen reminds me a dozen times a day — but I'm not. At breakfast I told Luella that Father would be home soon. Mrs. Owen pursed her lips.

"You cannot count on that, girl," she said to me.

"He will come home," I told her.

"More men die out there than make it back alive," she said. "He should never have gone and left his family to fend on their own."

I had no answer to that, as it is with shame I admit I have had similar criticisms of Father in my heart. He shouldn't have left us.

I saw Mrs. Sinclair tending the breakfast fire in front of her tent. With her English name and Indian face, she moves freely among both the Indian population and the white folk. The white women mostly ignore her, though Mama would nod and speak with her. There is a large encampment of Indians outside the fort. I used to fear them, but realize now they mean no harm. It angered me greatly to hear Mrs. Owen tell the ladies of the fort how *she* nursed Mama, when in reality it was Mrs. Sinclair with her potions and cool cloths who helped. I thought to ask her about laundry work, but a deep weariness steered my feet towards the river instead.

The morning air was clear, but with a chill. It is barren here, the land around the settlement stripped of its trees, but still it holds a particular beauty that satisfies me. As ducks rose from the river to take flight against the pink-gold morning sky, my fingers suddenly remembered charcoal and paper. I had done many sketches back home in Canada West, but have no spare paper to use here. It was just a passing fancy, gone as soon as the ducks vanished from sight.

May 29, 1862

I was frightened nearly out of my wits today as a volley was fired from every rifle in the fort and was soon answered from the river. I thought perhaps we were under attack, but it was the steamship *International* arriving, on her maiden voyage. Indians ran along the riverbank firing rifles in welcome. The boat was filled with men hoping to seek their fortunes in the Cariboo gold fields. More arrived this past week by stagecoach and cart. Gold! Gold and more gold — that is all they talk about! It is like a sickness with them. One that Father caught.

Many have come from Canada West, even some from the London area, near where we used to live, including two brothers, Joe and Henry Morgan. I asked if they remembered us, or our mill. Joe — the younger, I guess him to be about eighteen years of age — screwed up his face, rolled his eyes and gave every appearance of painful deep thought. Henry, the elder, shook his head impatiently at his brother, and growled that they didn't know my family.

The men are encamped outside the fort and number well over a hundred. One wandered about the settlement with a sketchbook in hand. I asked a soldier who he was. He said the man was a gentleman named William George Richardson Hind — and he is an artist! A real artist! I followed him as he walked a little distance, then stood and stared out over the prairie, chomping on a pipe, and drawing with quick strokes on paper. He looks a bit of a dandy with a balding head, eyeglasses and a short beard. Unfortunately, as I was sneaking up to catch a glimpse of his drawing, he turned his stare from the prairie to me! I quickly fled.

May 30, 1862

I heard Luella call Mrs. Owen *Mama* today. I shook her hard and told her she was never to call Mrs. Owen that again. Luella began to cry and said Mrs. Owen had told her to call her that. I felt sorry for my anger, and pulled Luella onto my lap, reminding myself it is not her fault. After all, she is only four.

May 31, 1862

I have a plan! Mama would not approve, but I positioned myself to overhear the men talking of the gold fields. Mrs. Sinclair was also there, collecting clothes for washing, but I believe she listened also. The men spoke of the cost of provisions, the route to follow, and the merits of a guide to lead them to Fort Edmonton. These discussions go on without end and I think they'd better decide soon or they will spend all summer talking about it. Or worse, I might lose the courage to follow my plan!

June 2, 1862, evening

I cannot believe my daring. Though worn out from fear and excitement, I am wide awake, wrapped in a blanket under a star-strewn sky on the prairie!

On my way to Cariboo! How is that for a dramatic start, dear diary? I have decided to bring you along to record my adventures for William and Luella. I can just see myself sitting with them, snug by a warm hearth while a winter wind howls outside, their eyes huge with astonishment at my tales. But that is for later.

My plan was to ask to go with the company to Cariboo to find Father, and bring him back to William and Luella. But that plan changed when I heard one man say no "petticoats" were to go on the journey. (Though Mrs. Schubert — definitely a petticoat — is travelling with her husband and three children, but that is yet another story for later.)

What was I to do? My brain was in a burning turmoil, when I came up with an even better plan. And only two days to prepare! I shortened a pair of Father's old pants, turned up the cuffs of an old woollen shirt I found in Mama's rag bag, and these, with a hat and stout boots of William's, turned me into a boy! I found two old packs amongst Mama's belongings from our trip west. Here is what I put into them:

a pot, a skillet, a water pouch, a plate, a cup, a fork, a skinning knife, needle and thread, a change of underclothing, an extra shirt (also rescued from the rag bag, with holes in the elbows) a ten-pound sack of flour, beans and dried apples from the store (which I plan to repay back *twice* over their price to Mrs. Owen when I return with Father and gold), a pound of baking soda (our own), some ink and a pen wrapped in a waterproof cloth, and of course you, dear diary. I fastened two blankets to the bottom of the pack for sleeping. It is heavy, my pack, but bearable. I have no choice anyway, because I have no cart (which with oxen costs $40.00!) to carry my things. At least I do not need miners' tools like picks and shovels as the rest of the travellers do. I wish I had pemmican, but had no money to buy some from the pemmican store. I spent a long time trying to decide whether or not to take Mama's wedding ring and watch. They are the only items of value I possess. Finally I sewed the ring into the waistband of my pants and buried Mama's watch in the bottom of the bag. I will use them only if necessary.

This morning — was it really only this morning? — I changed my clothes in a grove of aspen and cut my hair to my shoulders. When I stepped out of the grove, I got such a shock as to nearly stop my heart! Mrs. Sinclair stood there. I thought she'd try to stop me, but instead she held out a hide sack.

"Pemmican," she said. "For your journey." She saw my surprise, and explained that she'd heard of Mrs. Owen's plans to take Luella and William, and seen me listening to the men. It seems Mrs. Sinclair doesn't miss much. Then, from around her shoulders she took a buffalo skin and handed that to me also. I just remembered! In my surprise, I forgot to thank her!

Next I found William at the store, and stole him right from under Mr. Owen's nose! Mr. Owen didn't know who I was in my hat and my boy's clothes, though William soon realized. I told him my plan and made him cross his heart and promise not to tell anyone, not even Luella, where I had gone — she might accidentally tell Mrs. Owen — until one week had passed. I told him to say that I was helping Mrs. Schubert at the tavern. And William, being William, was more worried about getting his hat back, than about me! I am sorry to do this to Luella, but I'm doing it to *keep* her, so I hope one day she will forgive me.

I joined the confusion of carts, oxen, horses, cattle and people, moving from group to group so no one would know that I didn't belong to anyone. As we are so large a party — ninety-seven carts! — we have split into three groups. By afternoon the first line of carts was haphazardly fashioned, prayers were said over us, and our journey began. And here I am, on my way to Cariboo and Father.

June 5, 1862
Long Lake

Mama's watch tells me it is two o'clock in the morning, dear diary, and we have just now made camp. I am so weary I can barely hold my pen. We walked many miles today. My shoulders soon let me know my packs and blankets were far too heavy, so I sidled up to a cart, and when no one was looking, threw my buffalo skin and the heavier of the packs onto the back. I figure the oxen are much stronger than I. I had a bit of a scare when I lost track of the cart in the dark, but I soon found it again and retrieved my pack and my buffalo blanket. I'm grateful for it now, covering the hard ground beneath me.

William's boots rub the skin from my heels. They are so sore, I am not sure if I can go on. We travelled such a distance because we had no water. Our guide, Mr. Charles Rochette, assured us drinking water was but three miles ahead. Eight miles later we still had found none. Being unfamiliar with prairie travel and believing our guide's word that there was water just ahead, no one had thought to bring any along. By midday my tongue was so swollen with thirst it filled my mouth. Eleven hours we travelled without a drink. It was when we heard bullfrogs that we knew we were saved. I threw myself flat upon my stomach and drank my fill of the lake. Mr. Rochette might have come to us highly recommended, but *I* do not think much of this guide.

Late morning

Talk! Talk! And more Talk. That is all the men do — wrangle and bicker, while the day wears on. I can't help but think that women would just have got on with the task at hand. How these men even got this far is a wonder to me! The first morning of our journey was one of great confusion. Oxen ran off with or without their drivers, carts overturned, goods spilled everywhere. It caused a great delay, but then I guess I have to remember that most of these men are clerks, school teachers, shopkeepers or dandies who had servants to take care of their needs.

At last they have chosen a leader, Mr. Thomas McMicking. He is one of the few men here who is clean-shaven. He has very large, dark eyes and looks a bit thin and reedy. Not at all what I think a leader should look like. It is expected to take two months to reach the gold fields. Right now the men are writing down rules. One causes me some worry. Every man is to pay one dollar for the guide. I hope no one asks me to pay, as I do not have any money.

I keep apart from the others, my head down. If I need to speak, it is with as few words as possible. I go from the head of the line to the middle and the back, picking a different cart each day on which to stow my buffalo skin and pack. So far no one has asked me where my father is. One boy has spoken to me a few times, but I don't encourage him, though he seems friendly. The second day on the trail he and Joe Morgan milked a farmer's cows that were alongside the trail and brought me a cup. I wonder what the farmer thought at evening milking to find his cows gone dry!

The only real difficulty I have encountered, apart from the weight of my pack and my sore heels, was the first night, after the carts were set in a triangle as protection against Indian attack. We were all within and a watch set, so I could not leave the camp. That is when I realized I had forgotten to relieve myself and now could not do so. To be caught would reveal my disguise. Mostly I have found small scrub a short distance off to hide me. I held my breath tightly all night!

June 6, 1862

I had a close call today. I stowed my buffalo skin and pack on a cart, but didn't retrieve them fast enough at the end of the day, and the two men who owned the cart saw me. Their names are John and Thomas Drummond. They were quite nasty about it, Thomas saying they had paid for the oxen to pull *their* provisions, not anyone else's. I told them I had mistaken their cart for my father's in the early morning gloom when we were packing to begin our day's travels. John Drummond, who is the younger of the two — he looks about seventeen or eighteen — threw my pack onto the ground. It opened and all my goods scattered.

June 7, 1862

My legs and feet hurt too much tonight to write. That doesn't make sense, but that is how it is.

June 8, 1862

A day of rest as it is Sunday. Some men wished to go on, but Mr. McMicking said no. As much as I want to hurry to find Father, dear diary, I am glad to sit still, and let my feet rest. The blisters on them are a frightful sight. I boiled some water in my pot and cleaned them as best I could. I'm sitting now with my boots off.

The men had a prayer service and sang a hymn to mark the day, but I kept apart. Ever since Mama died, I'm not too sure about prayers. Waves of sadness keep coming over me today. Missing Mama, missing William and Luella. I expect by now the Owens have discovered that the Schuberts have left and William has told them that I have, too. Every time a scout rides up in a cloud of dust I think it is someone from the fort come to fetch me. Or perhaps Mrs. Owen has said nothing about my going missing. No doubt she has told William and Luella that I am not coming back either, even though I swore to William that I would. I bet she told them I've been stolen by Indians, or drowned in the river. I hope William doesn't believe her, as I told him I'd be back with Father.

I do not mean to cause them worry, but I see now I probably have. Another of my faults that Mama often sighed over — leaping before I look. "Just like your Father," Mama would always say. Oh dear! A tear just dripped off my nose and smudged the ink. I must think of something else if I do not want to ruin my writing.

I thought it would seem odd to people to see a boy writing, so at first I did it in secret. But some of the men here keep journals, so I now write in the open.

I like this prairie very much. Long grasses ripple like waves towards the horizon, broken by groves of aspen and cottonwood. Delicate pink wild roses dot the land. Ducks take wing above us, and prairie chickens nestle in the short grasses. My fingers itch to draw. I wish Mr. Hind had come with our party, but he travels behind us.

The days are long, stretching well into the night hours on both ends. The men and oxen are now becoming more used to each other, so it does not take as long to get everything in order to start the day. We've had to change our travelling schedule to suit the oxen. They are a hardy animal, even tempered and well suited to this land, but they need to be fed and watered constantly. We wake early, at two o'clock in the morning, and travel a few hours before breakfast. (Though sometimes we are so weary from the journey that it takes us until four to get up!) After the animals have taken their fill we commence again for a couple of hours until our nooning. A long rest in the afternoon and we walk again until late at night, but despite being tired, there is still time for some music by the fire and

Later

I'm sorry, dear diary, for leaving so abruptly. It was not my fault. John Drummond, who is a bully if I ever saw one, passed by and suddenly grabbed William's hat from my head. He held it out of reach while I jumped up and down on my sore feet and tried to get it. Suddenly the boy who had given me the cup of milk was there. "Pick on someone your own size," he said.

By then a number of men had stopped what they were doing to watch, so John Drummond dropped my hat and stomped it into the dirt before leaving.

The boy picked it up and handed it to me. "Don't mind him," he said.

I snatched the hat from him. "I can take care of myself," I said as I dusted it off. I didn't mean to be rude, but I was terrified of all those eyes turned my way.

June 9, 1862, nooning

If there is anything more disgusting than pemmican, I don't know what it could be! I am eternally grateful to Mrs. Sinclair for giving it to me, but the smell alone makes me gag. Buffalo meat on its own would be welcome, but roasted and beaten into powder and with hot animal fat added, it tastes very different. And because it keeps a long time, I will be eating it for weeks.

I had a good laugh to see Talbot's face when he was trying to choke down some of his own. Talbot is the name of the boy who rescued me from John. He is sixteen years old. I rode this morning on his father's cart. Seeing me struggle to put on my boots, he asked, "Where is your father?"

I said he was ahead of us. It is only a part lie, dear diary, as Father really is ahead of us — already in the gold fields. Talbot thought I meant at the head of the line, of course, but I can't help what he thinks. Talbot then said my feet were a mess and I should ride on his father's cart. I told him no, but he insisted. Mama said I was the most stubborn person she knew, but she didn't know Talbot! He's as stubborn as I am. Maybe more, as I did end up on the cart. I only had one moment of horror. Talbot asked what my name was and without thinking, I said, "Harri—" then stopped myself instantly when I realized what I was about to say. He said, "Harry?" and as that was a boy's name I nodded yes. I guess I'm Harry now.

Evening

My bones feel like they have been jolted apart from riding in the cart, and my bottom is sore (though I didn't say that to Talbot), but my feet are grateful. Riding did give me time to look around. It is quite a sight to see this long procession of ninety-seven carts winding before and after me across the prairie. Joe Morgan walked with us a ways. To get away from his brother, he told us. Joe and Henry bicker non-stop. Never have I met two brothers so different. Joe mulls over his words for a long time before saying anything; Henry speaks quickly. Joe is fair, tall and bulky, with huge hands, while Henry is thin, dark and quick moving. At first I didn't say much, worried that Joe would recognize me as the girl who spoke to him at the fort, but he didn't seem to, so I began to relax. I told them the plains were a great sea and our carts were ships sailing upon it. Talbot looked at me as if I were quite daft, and said, "I guess I like the land well enough. It looks good for farming." He and his Father had a farm near Goderich, back in Canada West.

These Red River carts are a strange affair. They carry 800 lbs. each and are constructed wholly of wood without a nail or piece of iron in sight. They are held together with wooden pegs, and rawhide, and therefore are supposedly easy to repair. The wheels shriek piercingly as they turn, and drivers shout and oxen bellow. My ears ache all the time here. We certainly will not sneak up on anyone.

Another strange affair is the basket cradle Mrs. Schubert has on her saddle horse to carry two of her three children. Gus is five, Mary Jane is nearly four and Jimmy is two. The Schuberts have brought their own Democrat carriage rather than a cart, as Mrs. Schubert thought it more comfortable for the journey.

Mrs. Schubert is the only petticoat allowed to travel with the men. Talbot said that Mr. Schubert was determined to go, and Mrs. Schubert was just as determined to accompany him. Talbot says that Mrs. Schubert is not a woman to be trifled with, but that it is his belief that women should not be travelling to Cariboo, as they have not the stamina. Obviously I could not speak my mind on *that*.

As we formed camp, Joe came up to me and said he could see how the prairie seemed like a sea. He'd obviously thought about it all day.

June 14, 1862
Fort Ellice

We have forded many streams but none with banks as steep as this. It is a magnificent sight, though, the green valley and the sparkling waters of the Qu'Appelle River and Beaver Creek, with Fort Ellice high on a hill opposite, but such a job to get to it. I told Talbot I had to help my father, then went a little ways off and sat in a grove of trees, and watched the carts be lowered by rope to the waiting scow. Two tipped over and all the goods were strewn about, and had to be packed again. The scow can only take one cart and animal at a time, so it is a lengthy job. Men draw the scow back and forth by rawhide ropes tied on either side of the river. Once on the other bank of the river, the carts have to be hauled up again. I will help Mrs. Schubert with the children and cross with her, as I do not want Talbot to see that I am alone.

June 15, 1862

We stayed today at the fort as it is Sunday. Like most Sundays we had services in the morning with scripture readings and hymns, but I still don't feel very pious. In fact, I wish I could use some of the words the men use to move an ornery ox, that is how mad I am! I thought to take the time to wash out my dirty shirt and underclothing and found a quiet spot by the river. Just as I bent over, a tremendous push from behind sent me headfirst into the water. John Drummond! Now both my shirts are soaking. Talbot asked why didn't I just take my shirt off and leave it to dry in the sun. I glared at him until he shrugged and went off, then I started a small fire. I am sitting in front of it as I write, to dry myself.

June 16, 1862

Rain! Rain! Rain! We have delayed our journey. I made biscuits and Talbot said they were the best he'd ever tasted. I told him I often helped my mother with the cooking. He looked at me quite strangely. I must be careful to think before I speak!

We had a music evening last night. There is quite an assortment of instruments travelling with us: mouth organs, clarinets, flutes, violins and a concertina. Joe was singing at the top of his voice as he always does. Henry sat a long time groaning, then finally burst out, "My horse farting sounds better than your singing! Begging your pardon, Ma'am." (That was for Mrs. Schubert.)

Talbot rolled all over the ground laughing. It was a mean thing for Henry to say, but I must admit Joe cannot carry a tune.

Evening

The rain let up at noon, so we left the fort, but immediately had a mishap. Mr. Morrow's ox ran away down the slope of the Qu'Appelle River, dragging Mr. Morrow behind him. The cart ran over Mr. Morrow's head. He lay there lifeless, but Dr. Stevenson saw to him and said Mr. Morrow will be up and about in a couple of days. Dr. Stevenson said the rain saved Mr. Morrow's life because when the wheel ran over his head, the head sank into the mud and that is what saved him.

Then John Drummond was leading his ox down the slope and it got away from him and overturned their cart, spilling their provisions everywhere. Thomas's face was like a thundercloud as he yelled at John.

Talbot asked me today to point out which man was my father. I pointed up the line and said the man with the hat. He asked, "Which one?" (They all wear hats). And I said, "The grey hat," in an exasperated voice that discouraged him from asking further in case he appeared a dolt.

June 18, 1862

We awoke this morning to find ice on the water buckets and the ground white with frost. We are delayed again as our guide, Mr. Rochette, has not shown up. I don't think Mrs. Schubert minds the delay. I crept away to relieve myself and saw she had done the same, but to be sick. I lay down in the grass as Mrs. Schubert passed so she would not see me. I saw something else while out in the grass, dear diary — John's brother, Thomas, giving him a beating with the oxen's whip. At first I felt quite happy to see John getting back what he gives, but as it went on I became uneasy. Father once gave William a sound whipping, but his arm did not strike as hard or as often as Thomas Drummond's did.

June 19, 1862

The guide never came back! The men are afraid that if he does turn up, it will be with a raiding party of Indians! We've heard such dreadful stories of Indians raiding and stealing goods, but decided to continue on our way alone, though every man has his rifle near at hand. I jump at every sound, expecting war cries and arrows! Talbot told me to go stay with my father, so I moved up the line a little and walked with Joe. Keeping a falsehood is very hard work!

June 22, 1862

It is Sunday. A day of rest. I no longer feel sorry for John. Today he kicked over my pan of biscuits as they cooked on the fire at noon. I have so little food, I was beside myself with fury and I almost called him a word I heard Mr. Dyer call his oxen yesterday. I bit my tongue, dear diary. I don't think Mama would approve of some of the men's language, but I can't help hearing it, can I? I try quite hard to let it go in one ear and out the other, but some of the words seem to stick in between. I do notice that the men bite their tongues around Mrs. Schubert. I expect Mr. Schubert's tongue must be fair bitten through! I don't know why John torments me so. I've done nothing to him. He does leave me alone when Talbot is around, as he and Talbot are of a size, but Talbot hasn't been around much, as I've tried to keep more to myself since letting it slip that I helped Mama cook. I can't have anyone finding out my secret, as I know they'd leave me at one of the forts we pass. Maybe I'll stick close to Joe instead. He's even bigger than Talbot.

My feet have healed and hardened and my legs

no longer ache as much at the end of each day's march. Most days we make 20 miles and on a good day, 30. I am afraid I am going to run out of food, so I limit myself to one meal a day and I am so hungry by evening that even my pemmican tastes good. I have discovered it's tolerable if fried. My big news, though, is that I found a way to earn a bit of money. I noticed Mr. Bailey flailing about with a shirt in the river as he tried to wash it, but he lost his grip on it and it floated away. I fished it out and asked him if he'd like me to do his wash for him. He said, "Gladly." I do laundry for him now and for a few of the other men. It feels good to have some money in my pocket.

We have gone through some lovely country of open plains, groves of poplar, wild roses and lakes teeming with ducks. Some of the men complain of the sameness of the land, but if you look close, it is very different. Mrs. Schubert was unwell yesterday and prone in her carriage so I let Gus Schubert walk with me to give her some peace. I tried to show him some of the differences I saw in the land, but he was more interested in gathering buffalo chips. I let him, as I needed them for my fire anyway, but then Mrs. Schubert kindly invited me to share dinner with her family. I told her I'd have to get permission from my father. I ran up the line of carts a bit, waited a few minutes and came back. The idea of the prairie as an ocean and our carts as vessels upon it has stayed with me. I shall make a small sketch of what I see in my mind. Nothing as grand as the real artist Mr. Hind would do, but something to keep the memory.

June 24, 1862

The more I wear them, the more I like these boy's clothes. I used to tie my skirts up so my legs would be freer, but with trousers, my strides are longer and I can run faster without a skirt tangling about my legs.

As we passed through the Touchwood Mountains, I noticed strawberries growing beside our path. I gathered a pan-full. Talbot said they were as plentiful and as easy to pick as gold nuggets are from the riverbanks in Cariboo. I asked him how he knew that, and he said it was common knowledge that in Cariboo, gold was just lying around ready for the picking. I sniffed my disbelief and he became quite huffy and left me to myself for the afternoon. I didn't mind at all because that is all he talks about — gold! The same gold that made Father leave us.

Thinking of that makes tears sting behind my eyes. Mama didn't want to leave our home at all, even when it was just for land in the west. "No woman wants to be travelling," she told me. "She wants to be settled." But Father hankered after wider spaces, and new things for his eyes to see. He told Mama the mill was his father's dream, not his, and so he decided to sell up, and despite Mama's grumbles about dreamers and restless feet, we found ourselves at Fort Garry. I will share my strawberries with Mrs. Schubert. She's looking a bit peaky. Besides, they have a milk cow for the children, so hopefully there will be cream to go with our berries.

June 25, 1862
Quill Plains

We cross the Quill Plains. Not a tree to ease our eyes or shade us from the hot sun beating down from a wide blue sky. The very air appears to shimmer from the heat. I've been wearing my coat to save me carrying it, but today am forced to take it off. My pack slips on the sweat on my back and is rubbing my skin raw. The ground here is littered with buffalo skulls. We were told at Fort Garry that there would be buffalo on the trail for food, but we have yet to see a live one. Joe says seeing all the skulls makes him feel uneasy, like walking through a graveyard, but Henry told him not to be so foolish. I know what he means though, as the yellow bones stretching as far as the eye can see make me uneasy, too.

Evening

I was stumbling about in a heat daze when Joe suddenly picked me up and tossed me and my pack onto the back of his and Henry's cart. He said I looked like I was going to fall flat on my face. I was glad for the ride, but not so glad when Henry asked after my father. I put him off, but I fear, dear diary, I'll soon be found out.

A black cloud of mosquitoes descended on us this evening, biting people and animals alike. We got the fires going quickly so the smoke would drive them away. I overheard one of the men say that a woman back at Fort Garry killed herself, she was so plagued by mosquitoes. I can almost believe that! The smoke helped, but not much. I am covered with bites.

June 26, 1862, midday meal

It is quite a funny sight. Each morning there is a race by the men to see who will be at the head of the line. With cups of tea and plates of pancakes they run about packing their camps up. Some do not even bother to pack their tents, but run around with dishes in their arms in an attempt to be first in the line. There is, though, an advantage to being first, as the dust is thick at the back, and if there is a mudhole, it is so big by the time the last carts come along, the wheels get stuck fast in it and must be pulled out. Henry grumbles bitterly about this race, yet this morning he threw his goods every which way into his cart and yelled at Joe, "Move, you big lout! You're slower than an ox."

June 27, 1862

I am near driven frantic by mosquitoes! They sing about my ears, land on my eyes and torment me with their stings. The Schubert children cry bitterly and the animals suffer greatly, too. I bite my tongue so I do not scream!

June 30, 1862
Fort Carlton

I cannot believe we've come so far! Yet some of the men complain that we've not gone fast enough. I think it a great distance, especially as I walked most of the way! I have the blisters to prove it.

We almost had a drowning today, though. We reached the South Saskatchewan River early this morning. The Hudson Bay Company boat was on the opposite shore from us so two of the men swam over and towed it back. The wheels were taken off the carts, the animals unharnessed, and the loads removed to be ferried across the river. The cattle and horses were made to swim. Some were reluctant and Mr. Kelso entered the river to hurry them on and the current swept him away. Three men plunged in to rescue him. They had a time of it, but dragged him limp onto the bank. We all watched anxiously as they pummelled his back and chest. Finally he coughed, was violently sick, and was saved. I bet he's wondering if he should ever have left Acton. John said if I'd fallen in, he would have let the river have me. Talbot assured me *he* would rescue me. I stuck my tongue out at John. It's quite fun at times being a boy.

July 4, 1862

Yesterday we passed through the Thickwood Hills and today through the Lumpy Hills. Aren't those funny names, dear diary?

Because of my laundry money, I was able to buy more pemmican and a pair of moccasins at Fort Carlton. My feet will welcome the change from my boots from time to time.

July 6, 1862

I have been found out! And all because of strawberries! The land west of Fort Carlton is quite different from the plains — hilly, with many streams, and thick with strawberries. I filled my pan with them, and then my old pemmican bag. As it was Sunday, Talbot was picking with me and grumbling about the slowness of the job. Without thinking I said, "It's easier if you just fold your apron, and put in the strawberries as you pick, then dump them in a basket. It goes much faster." I suddenly realized what I'd said. "That's what my mother did. That's what I meant," I quickly added, but my face was red and my tongue fell all over the words. At first I thought Talbot believed me, since we picked for a few more minutes in silence, then he said he'd like to meet my father. I told Talbot he was having a nap.

"He has to wake sometime," Talbot said.

I said he'd be busy with the oxen, but the excuses sounded weak even to my ears, and finally I ran out of them.

"My father isn't here," I finally confessed and, much to my dismay, burst into tears — just like a girl! I told Talbot how Mama had died and Father was in the gold fields and I was going to find him and how Mrs. Owen wanted to take Luella and William back to Toronto. It was supper by the time I had finished my tale. Then Talbot said, "And you're not a boy, are you?"

I had hoped he'd forgotten my apron story while I talked, but he hadn't. I admitted I wasn't a boy. "What's your real name?" he asked. I told him it was Harriet, and pleaded with him not to tell anyone. He is thinking about it right now, dear diary. I am near beside myself with worry. If he tells, I'll be left at the next fort. I will make him some pancakes with strawberries to help him think.

July 9, 1862
Fort Pitt

We are at Fort Pitt. From here, we are told, the trail grows more difficult. Talbot still hasn't made his decision and I am in a burning turmoil. But, I have decided, even if he tells and I'm left behind, I'll find my *own* way to the gold fields.

Later

Talbot has decided. He told his father that my father was already at Cariboo and that I was alone. BUT he did not tell his father I was a girl. He said he didn't tell because he was so used to me being Harry, he didn't want to have to learn to call me Harriet. Mr. Dyer said I could travel with them. I was so excited I almost hugged Talbot, then remembered boys don't do that, but still, I was that happy. Mr. Dyer also said I could put my buffalo skin and packs on their cart. Talbot really is the nicest person. He told me his mother died when he was fourteen. He has no brothers or sisters. He said that he and his father heard about the gold finds and as they didn't have any family to hold them back, left their farm in their neighbour's care and decided to come west to see for themselves.

John dragged one of my blankets through a mud puddle!

July 10, 1862

We are staying a day at the fort as the men want to hire a guide — one that won't desert us! The trail is not well marked and the Blackfeet Indians caught a party of white men only three days ago, stripped them naked and sent them back! I pray that doesn't happen to us, as then I would surely be found out by all. Talbot and his father have cleaned their guns. I find I am quite nervous today between worrying about Indian attacks and waiting to see what John will do to me. It seems cowardly, but I stick close to Talbot. Too close, maybe. I nearly walked right up his back when he stopped quite abruptly a few minutes ago.

We are greatly bothered by dogs here — well, really they are more like wolves. During the summer the fur traders leave the dogs to their own devices, so the animals are starving. They come right into camp at night and steal our food. I sleep with my pemmican tucked under my arm, though I do worry the dogs might tear my arm off to get the food, but I don't know what else to do.

July 12, 1862

Spent all day in camp. I am wet through and through. And also covered in mud! All because of John. It looked like the weather would break, so we set off from the fort, but soon stopped, due to more rain and thick fog hiding the trail. For two days it has stormed with great winds and silver sheets of water. As I was climbing up a muddy incline yesterday, John suddenly appeared out of the rain and kicked my feet out from under me. I went tumbling backwards, right beneath the hooves of a horse. Somehow I managed to roll away before they came down on me, but I landed in a marshy area that the rain had turned to a huge mud lake! Joe fished me out and set me on my feet. I am so cold now my teeth chatter without stop, but it is too wet for a fire.

Wolves follow us day and night and howl unceasingly, sending shivers up my spine and making everyone sharp-tongued from lack of sleep. Why did I think I could make it to the gold fields? I miss Luella and William. I do not think I am adequate to this task. Cannot write anymore as the rain is dripping on my page and making the ink run!

July 13, 1862

It's Sunday, so we're staying at camp another day. All in all it has not been a good day. The ground is muddy and everything is wet — tents, clothes. Talbot has gone to see if he can find some dry wood, but I doubt there is any. Everyone is short-tempered. Thomas Drummond got into a fist-fight with another man. It reminded me of school back home — the two fighters, the ring of people urging them on and the more sensible ones pulling them apart.

Then Thomas told John he was useless because John couldn't start a fire. Can't he see that *nobody* can start a fire? And then, dear diary, Henry and Joe started arguing. Henry complained that Joe was slowing them down so they never made the head of the line in the mornings, and that he ate too much and they'd soon run out of food. Joe told Henry to stop being so bossy. Then Henry said, "I wish I'd never brought you with me."

"Well, I wish I'd never come," Joe said. Then added, "Besides, I'd rather look at my ox's arse than your face any old day. Begging your pardon, Missus." That last was to Mrs. Schubert. I wouldn't normally write *that* word, dear diary, except it is exactly what he said. It certainly shut Henry up. In fact, it shut all of us up, as that was very quick thinking for Joe. Henry's face was brilliant red with anger.

Mrs. Schubert's face was red, too, but I think it was from holding in her laughter.

Later

A scout just came back and said there is a party of Blackfeet in the hills west of us. Extra guards are being posted for the night!

July 14, 1862

We awoke safe and sound. John's antics are fast becoming tiresome. If he is not taking my hat or spilling my food, he is tripping me or pushing and shoving me into mudholes. To think I almost felt sorry for him yesterday.

July 15, 1862

We came upon five dead Blackfeet and Cree. There had obviously been a fierce battle between them. We went on, rifles ready, but didn't see any live Indians. I'm so scared.

July 18, 1862

We are all miserable. Rain plagues us daily, and the sloughs and rivers have swollen to become acres of marsh. I wade most of the day through water up to my waist! I will never be dry again! The carts and oxen become mired frequently and must be pulled out. We barely make any distance. Even John has no energy to play his tricks. Joe and Henry are still not speaking to each other.

July 20, 1862

Sunday. Half the men are working and the other half are grumbling — about the men who are working. They are building yet another bridge. The pious ones charge the others with breaking the Sabbath, but the need to build bridges has slowed our progress considerably. Mr. Sellar says that the bridges being made run anywhere from 40 to 100 feet long. The rivers are so swollen by rain that we can't ford them.

I find it interesting how the bridges are built. Trees are felled on the river banks, then some men swim across the river, towing the largest trees to the other side, where they are fastened. They do this again and again, until the width is enough to support a cart. I rather expect, though, that those who stand and watch and exchange harsh words will use the Sunday-built bridge come tomorrow morning.

Mr. Dyer asked what I thought of a bridge being built on the Lord's Day. Not being pious myself — especially since Mama and the baby died — I told him I didn't think the Lord would mind this once. He laughed and handed Talbot and me axes and told us to cut some smaller trees. Talbot protested that I shouldn't chop, but I felled *him* with one sharp look. "I *have* chopped wood before," I said, then wore myself out flailing away at small trees to prove myself as good as any boy.

July 22, 1862
Fort Edmonton

We have arrived at Fort Edmonton. We are camped opposite it until we can ferry across the North Saskatchewan River. The fort's boat is lost downstream due to the flooding, so the men have gone in search of it. Eleven days of rain! But today it is very fine; the air fresh, the sky blue with fluffy clouds. To get here we crossed the steepest river-bank yet on this journey — a ravine 200 feet deep, says Mr. Sellar. (Mr. Sellar likes spouting figures; I like to listen, though I did not like arithmetic at school back home!) A trail was opened through the brush by axes, and the carts and cattle were let down by ropes on one side, and moved across a bridge the men had made. Then all were pulled up again on the other side. A long and difficult job. I remember the men back at Fort Garry saying the prairie is easily travelled. I begin to think they never made the journey!

I made myself quite useful today, mending mine, and Talbot's, and his father's clothes. I also baked biscuits. I shook out blankets and cleaned pots until Talbot finally said, "We're not going to leave you behind, so stop it." I wonder how he knew I was worried about that.

July 24, 1862

I rounded a corner of the barracks and came upon John, crying. I stopped, unsure whether or not to let him know I was there. All of a sudden he looked up and saw me. He dashed his hand across his eyes and pushed roughly past me. He didn't say anything, but the look he gave me sent a shiver down my spine.

I told Talbot about it. He said Thomas had been slapping John earlier and telling him he was of no use. Talbot also said John would be mad that I had seen him crying, as it would hurt his pride, and that

I should be careful. It is funny, dear diary, but it is like I saw Talbot for the first time today. He has yellow brown hair, like wheat ready to be harvested, and eyes that can be blue or grey depending on the colour of the sky behind him.

July 25, 1862

Woke up this morning with a stomach full of butterflies. What if I get to Cariboo and cannot find Father? What if the Owens take Luella and William to Toronto earlier than they said? What if I never find them again? What if I run out of food and starve? Or become ill? On and on my worries go. It is as if I was too busy to worry before, but now that we are in one place for a few days, they've all heaped on my head. I have a little bit of tea in payment for washing clothes. I've been hoarding it, but today I need it!

Afternoon

A cup of tea and a bath in the river have chased the worries away — for now. I know they are there waiting to attack me again in a weak moment.

Talbot came up this afternoon, and with a very red face asked if I would like to have a bath. "I'll keep watch," he said, then his eyes widened and he began to stammer. "I mean, not watch you, I mean, I'll watch for other people. Who might see you. Except, they won't see you. Because I'll keep watch." I had a hard time not grinning. I thought about it for a minute, and decided I would very much like a bath. At first it was awkward walking to the river together, so I gave him a good shove into a prickly rose bush. Then he was mad instead of embarrassed and we were fine again.

July 26, 1862
Still Fort Edmonton

We are staying here a few days while the men decide which route to choose. Mr. Dyer is not favourably impressed with the fort. He says it is poorly run. It is very dirty, both the fort and the people. All of them — half-breeds, Indians and whites! The place abounds with starving dogs that make our lives a misery. They snarl and snap, quite ferocious. John threatened to feed me to them, but Talbot was beside me so all he could do was threaten. Mrs. Schubert seems quite relieved to be in one place for a few days. She is taking in washing, too, but there is more than enough for both of us. We spent most of the day at the river with soap, and then spread the clothes on bushes to dry. My hands are very red now, but the cleanest they've been under the nails in weeks!

July 27, 1862

My pemmican is gone! Mr. Dyer said the dogs must have got it but I know it was John! I saw him skulking around earlier. I marched right up to him and yelled, "You took my pemmican, didn't you?" I wasn't even scared of him, I was so furious. He pretended he didn't know what I was talking about! I *know* he did it.

July 28, 1862

I bought some flour from the store with my laundry money and gave it to Mr. Dyer, saying it was to pay him for sharing his cart. At first he didn't want to take it, but Talbot nudged him with an elbow and then he did. It is a good thing I had that money, because I was able to replace my pemmican. Who would have thought at the beginning of this journey that I would look forward to a bite of pemmican! I did a lot of washing for Mr. Hunter today and he gave me a new pair of moccasins in return. I was glad to get them, as my old pair has a hole in the heel. I had hoped to have a bit of money left over to sew into my waistband beside Mama's wedding ring, but prices are quite dear here. At least I've not had to trade the ring or the watch for goods. Just thinking about that brings a sharp pain to my chest and a lump into my throat. I miss Mama so much. I best think of something else.

We are to continue on our journey tomorrow morning. I'm very relieved to go. It has been a rest, and there have been many enjoyable evenings of music and story-telling, but I worry the entire time that someone other than Talbot will find out I am a girl. This fort is the last place I could be left behind before the mountains.

There has been endless discussion between the men in our party and the men at the fort about the best trail over the mountains, but finally they decided to head to Tête Jaune Cache. Some men say it is not the easiest route, but there is talk of an easy trail from there, or as one man calls it, a road to Cariboo.

Most of the carts are sold now, though a few of the men kept theirs, and many of the oxen traded for horses. Mr. Dyer kept his, as he felt oxen would make the trek over the mountains easier than horses. Everything must be packed on the backs of the animals or carried by us. Mr. Dyer said the trading for provisions was the most bothersome part of the entire journey, as the fur-traders and the half-breeds change their prices minute to minute. I left a letter here to be taken to Fort Garry to William, so he'll know I am all right and he can reassure Luella.

July 29, 1862

We are on our way again to Cariboo! We will be there in a few weeks! I am so glad. The fort was beginning to smell quite ripe, between all the people and animals. We are to take the Tête Jaune Pass. A guide has been hired — André Cardinal. Some say the Tête Jaune Pass is the more difficult because of trees fallen on the trail, but quicker. The way I see it, the faster I can get to Father, the better!

Night

It took a little longer than expected to set out. We go by pack train now rather than cart, and the oxen did not appreciate having pack saddles placed upon their backs. As fast as we put the loads on, the oxen shook them off. I helped Talbot, though I kept a close watch on the oxen's feet, as they were not shy about knocking us about with their hooves. There are a hundred and forty mules, horses and oxen now. A Mr. Felix Munroe has been hired to pack extra supplies for us, as there is no room left on our own animals. Because we took so long to prepare, we only went 10 miles to the settlement of St. Albert.

August 1, 1862
St. Anne's Mission

I'm exhausted. Struggled through mud up to my knees, and climbed over fallen trees and through thickets. Six men with axes went ahead, chopping a trail through the bush, but the trees stand so thick we had to pass single file. Then we came to a swamp: black mud sucking at our feet, and submerged roots tripping us and twining about the horses' hooves and needing to be cut away so they can move. The oxen do better here than horses. Those who refused to give up their carts soon regretted it, as the carts are frequently mired past their axles and it is quite a job to get them out. Never have I felt so glad to see a place as this small settlement of St. Anne's. I barely had the strength to help Talbot unload our packs from the oxen.

Which reminds me, dear diary. Talbot is becoming tiresome. He rushes to my aid, won't let me lift the packs. When no one was within hearing, I whispered to him to stop treating me like I was fine china!

"But you're a girl," he whispered back. It was a forward thing to do, but I pulled back my shirt-sleeve and exposed my arm nearly to the shoulder and bent it to show him the muscle there. He turned a most interesting red that climbed right up his neck to his face and set his ears on fire.

I think Mrs. Schubert was glad to rest here also. It was a horrible day. At one point, little Gus fell off his horse and was nearly trampled by the one behind him. It almost stopped my heart, so I know Mrs. Schubert's must have stopped altogether!

And Mrs. Schubert's horse couldn't bear her weight in the swamp, so she had to wade through the mud in her long skirts, grasping the children's hands and pulling them along. Then Mary Jane fussed until I took her with me. I entertained her for a bit with some stories that I had told Luella, then she fussed again and I returned her to her mother. I wanted to tell Mrs. Schubert that trousers are much easier to walk in than skirts, but couldn't quite figure out how without revealing I am a girl!

It is pretty, this St. Anne's. It's a mission and set-tlement on the shores of a beautiful lake. The fields are tilled and ripe berries are everywhere for the picking. Smoke curls from the fires of a small encampment of half-breeds, all watched over by a little church. There are three priests and at least that many nuns, the first white women we have seen since we left Fort Garry. One of the nuns does not appear to be much older than myself! One of the men travelling with us called the nuns slaves of Satan — he does not like Catholics. He states very loudly to anyone who'll listen that he is Protestant. I am Protestant myself, but I do not see any tails or horns here — except on the oxen!

I want to go into the church. You see, dear diary, I am forgetting Mama — her face, her voice — and I'm scared I'll lose her entirely. I thought perhaps being inside a church would make me feel closer to her, help me remember. But I don't know if Catholics will let Protestants into their church and I am afraid to ask.

Poor Mr. Morrow, whose head was run over before, got kicked in the face today by his ox! He is to stay at St. Anne's until he recovers. If I were him, I would think twice about continuing to Cariboo!

August 2, 1862

The trail becomes more difficult. As before, six men go ahead of us and cut through brush and trees to clear a path. The going is slow. Muddy ground sucks at our feet, making each step torture. My legs ache constantly, but after showing Talbot my arm muscle, I certainly cannot complain. The horses are not doing well. They become mired down easily and the men carry the horses' packs! The oxen continue to do better. We are leaving quite a trail of belongings behind us — valises, clothing, pots — as many try to lighten their load.

August 3, 1862

I am so tired and sore. I will never make it to the gold fields. I should never have come! I want to go home! I want to be back in our house by the mill!

August 4, 1862

Mr. Dyer is not well. We are camped beside the Pembina River. This river is deep and rapid and roars in my ears. The men are trying to decide how to ford it. A hill next over to us is smoking! At first some men thought it to be a volcano, but it is a smouldering seam of coal. Talbot is caring for his father, so I have gathered enough of the coal to build a large fire to warm him. It is very quiet, with only the sound of rushing water to fill the silence. No one has the strength to talk.

August 5, 1862

When we woke this morning it was cold. Heavy dew had frozen and hung in icicles from the trees, sparkling in the morning sun. Talbot and I packed up as Mr. Dyer rested. He shivers constantly and has a bad cough. Mama would have put a mustard plaster on his chest. Dr. Stevenson has dosed him with some syrup and Mr. Dyer said it did him wonders, but I couldn't see any improvement in him.

This guide has proven a good one. He showed the men how to take the tents, stretch them on the ground and put all the supplies into them. Then he folded the tops together and tied them shut with a rope. Horses towed the bundles across the river. Talbot and I crossed behind an ox, holding a rope tied to its harness, up to our neck in water. Mr. Dyer rode a horse across, but he might as well have swum as he got so wet. It just about did him completely in.

August 6, 1862

Mr. Dyer got up this morning, walked for about an hour, then fell down and could not get back up. He, Talbot and I are camped here on the only patch of dry ground we could find in the swamp. Talbot urged me to go on with the others, but I didn't feel right leaving them. They have been kind to me. Besides, there are many stragglers spread out along the trail, so we can join up with one of them when Mr. Dyer is well. At least that is what I tell myself when my stomach gets butterflies. The truth is, I'm very afraid of being left behind to find our own way over the mountains without a guide.

It is so quiet here, just the three of us. The only sounds are rustling in the undergrowth, an occasional bird-call, the snuffling of oxen and Mr. Dyer's ragged coughing. Talbot is white-faced with worry. I told him a day's rest would set his father right, but I don't believe myself. I can't stand the silence, so I'm writing in you, dear diary, to keep my fears at bay. If only there were something to see! But tree branches hide the sky, thick woods press in from either side, mud is beneath our feet, and dark shadows are everywhere. I'm terrified of spending a night here.

August 7, 1862

Mr. Dyer still unwell! This afternoon I suddenly remembered one winter when I had a dreadful cough and Mama's remedy for it, so we decided to try it. We've built the fire quite high, and have boiled water in our largest pot. We then placed a blanket over both the pot and Mr. Dyer, so he could breathe in the steam. We are also making him drink many cups of weak tea. We will do this throughout the night and hope for the best.

August 8, 1862

We had a time of it, but Mr. Dyer is on the mend. This morning, as the queer green light filtered through the trees, I brought another cup of tea to Mr. Dyer, but he waved me off, sat up and said, "You have me fair swimming, boy!" That's when we knew he was on the mend. I think even Talbot and I were better for the enforced rest. We started off again, slowly, with frequent stops for Mr. Dyer to catch his breath. With the trail having been cleared by those in front of us, the going is easier.

I had one moment today that nearly stopped my heart. We came upon a grave! It said *James Doherty*. I couldn't breathe, as it suddenly occurred to me that this might be why I had not heard any more from Father other than his one letter. Perhaps he died in Cariboo and is buried in a grave such as this. The idea wormed its way inside my head and would not leave. I sniffed back tears for a long time after that until Mr. Dyer said that he hoped I was not catching his cold.

August 9, 1862

We have caught up to the main party.

August 10, 1862

All has been found out — by everyone, not just Talbot. They all know I am a girl! It is Sunday so we are camped for the day. I was writing in my diary this morning. A man walked by and asked what I was doing. I told him I was writing my memories of our journey. "You want to remember this?" he asked.

I told him that I did.

"Funny, I just want to forget it," he said. He walked away, and suddenly my diary was pulled from my hand. John!

He ripped a page of my precious paper out and let it float away in the wind. He started to rip a second one, when I saw red and ran at him and tackled him and knocked him to the ground, hands pummelling him. He easily shoved me away, and came at me with a fist. I rolled away, but not quick enough, and caught a clip on my ear. It stunned me, and I thought, I'm really in for it now. Then another body joined the fray and John went flying into the dirt. Talbot straddled him and yelled, "Don't you *ever* hit her again!" *HER!* That is what he said.

John scrambled to his feet and stared at me. "He's a *girl?*"

Talbot's face was a picture as he realized what he'd said. Under other circumstances, I would have quite enjoyed seeing it, but not now. Then, like wind whispering from tree to tree, I heard the words "a girl" pass through the camp. Mr. Dyer is furious at Talbot for lying, though I tried to explain to him that it was my fault.

Then, in front of the entire company, I was asked to speak up for myself and tell why I'd practised this deception. I imagine this is how it feels for a criminal to be before a court of law, faces and eyes upon him as he tells his tale.

I told them the entire story, about Father, Mrs. Owen, Luella and William, and Mama dying. A couple of the men wiped their eyes to hear of her passing, and I hoped they would speak up for me. John and Thomas Drummond said I should be sent back with Mr. Munroe, who is returning to Fort Edmonton tomorrow, as we no longer need him to pack supplies.

"Why does she have to go back?" Joe asked. "She's a sturdy little lad."

"That's just it," Henry told him, much exasperated. "*She's* not a lad! She's a girl!"

John said I would slow them all down, but Henry

pointed out that so far I'd kept up with no difficulty, and then went on to say, "And she gave you a fair wallop." There were a lot of smiles and snorts at that, though not from John or Thomas. I almost stuck my tongue out at him, but remembered in time that they knew I was a girl and I could no longer do that. They are still discussing my fate!

Evening

I am to continue on! Mrs. Schubert spoke up and said she'd have me travel with them. She told the men she thought it better than having me go back with the guide alone, and most agreed. I thanked the group and apologized, feeling very small indeed! Mrs. Schubert offered me a skirt of her own, but I told her I found the boy's clothes more to my suiting. She half-smiled, which made me think she'd prefer them, too.

August 11, 1862

We cross a river a day now; sometimes the very same river three or four times when we find the way blocked on one side or the other by windfall or rocks. The rivers have funny names — Root River, Buffalo Dung River. Some men swim across, some ride their horses. As I can't swim, I either get a ride or hold onto the tail of a horse and let myself be towed across. Unfortunately, it often means I am wet all day long. Our progress is slow. We are lucky to make 10 miles a day. The woods are thick and the only time we see something other than trees is when we come to a river. Talbot says he is growing tired of nothing to look at but the "arse" of the ox in front of him. Mr. Dyer told him to mind his language, with a meaningful glance at me. Now that I think about it, I realize all the men bite their tongue around me, the way they do Mrs. Schubert. It's too bad — I was acquiring quite a stock of what Mama would call "colourful words" to impress William.

Here it is almost two and a half months into our journey, and we are still in the mountains. I think now that those folks who told us we'd be in the gold fields in two months never travelled this way! I am thankful for our guide, as there is no apparent trail for us to follow, just occasional marks blazed into the bark of the trees to show our way. I doubt we would find them on our own. Our food is running low, so we are eating but two meals a day. Mrs. Schubert, I notice, often passes her portion to the children, which makes me feel quite guilty to be eating all mine myself, but I'm so hungry by the end of the day's march I can't help it.

August 13, 1862

No amount of imagining could prepare me for our first sight of the Rocky Mountains! We came out of a thick swamp today and there they were before us. White peaks against the blue sky, the lower slopes black with evergreens. Never have I seen anything so magnificent. I cannot even describe them to you, dear diary, as words seem so inadequate. Mr. McMicking says we are still 100 miles away, yet their snow-capped tops are clearly visible. I will try to sketch them to keep the memory, though I know my effort won't even begin to reflect their majesty. Most importantly, on the other side of the mountains is Father! It won't be long now.

August 14, 1862

A horse gave out today. Many other animals are very weak, as there is no pasturage for them. I am so hungry my stomach presses against my spine.

August 16, 1862

If I ever see home again, I swear I'll never stir from it!

August 17, 1862

Some of the men did not want to take our Sunday rest. There is little food and they thought to press on, but the majority won out and we are camped for the day. It is a good thing, as I am very tired. We are a threadbare looking group now; the men's beards unkempt, tears and holes in our clothes, both clothes and ourselves filthy from not having had a wash for a while. I'm proud to say I caught a fair number of trout in the river today, which I fried over the fire and shared, but still our provisions are very low, so we are on rations. It takes all our strength to travel, with none left over to hunt or fish by nightfall. It is, though, beautiful here, the mountains towering above us, the sky blue, the river flashing silver in the sun. There is little talk among the men, as most sit with their thoughts. I took out Mama's watch and held it close, remembering it pinned to her chest, pretending the steady tick was her heart yet beating.

Talbot has gone to see if he can find anything to shoot for the cooking pot, but there is a new strangeness between us that neither of us will talk about, so I feel doubly alone. I have been helping Mrs. Schubert with the children today, as I am trying not to put myself forward so the men won't regret letting me continue.

John walked by and made a point of kicking up stones with his feet to hit me as he passed, but I'm too tired to bother making a fuss.

August 19, 1862, morning

Got little sleep, as there was a fierce thunderstorm last evening. The worst I've ever seen. The sky darkened like night and lightning struck from peak to peak, while thunder rang in our ears and wind tore at our tents. Joe was quite wild-eyed with fear, which ordinarily would seem funny in such a big man, but it was a storm like none of us has experienced before, and we were all scared.

We go up and up, and at times the trail leads between towering walls of rock. One of the men said it made him right nervous having all that rock lean over top of him, and give him the open plains any day. Yet for others it is the wideness of the prairies that makes them nervous. André Cardinal gave us the choice of two routes to follow: the south side of the Athabaska River where the trail is steep and treacherous, or the north side, where the trail is better, but there are two deep rivers to swim. The men chose the south side. There are more non-swimmers than swimmers.

Evening
Jasper House

Never have I been so scared! All day we climbed up and up a steep, rocky trail with a sheer drop to the right of us. There was nothing to be seen but sky, a sight that made my heart flip and flop like a dying fish. Dumb old Talbot went right to the edge and looked over and told me to come and see, as the valleys were full of cornflowers and bluebells and Jasper House could be seen in the distance. I pretended an indifference, because my legs shook at the very thought of looking over that cliff! But I didn't want Talbot to know that. I took hold of the ox's tail, keeping well away from its feet, and let it pull me up. At places the trail was only a foot wide!

The packs on the animals rubbed against the rock walls, making them stagger about until finally Mr. Blanchard's horse missed its footing and hurtled down the trail on its back! It was a miracle that a tree broke its fall, as the drop is 900 feet! (Mr. Sellar told me that.) After watching that horse tumble, I thought perhaps it wiser to not hold onto the ox's tail! I closed my eyes so I wouldn't see all that sky, but then I stumbled over a rock and it was only Henry grabbing my arm quickly that saved me from going over the edge. Finally I looked straight ahead and muttered prayers for the rest of the day, — something I don't often do.

We passed Jasper House in the afternoon, a small, lonely looking, white-washed building with boarded-up windows. Mrs. Schubert was sorely disappointed it was abandoned, as she'd hoped to be able to trade for much needed food.

August 20, 1862

Slept last night on the flats near the Athabaska River. The mountain peaks looked beautiful, coloured pink and gold by the setting sun.

August 21, 1862

It seems the entire journey I have been wet at least once in the day. We forded the Athabaska River yesterday on rafts the men built, and waded and swam across the Miette River innumerable times today. Every day I wake to the sound of chopping, as the axemen get up at two in the morning to begin clearing the way for us. Joe, with his great strength, is a favourite of the men for this job. But despite their efforts, larger fallen trees block the trail so we cross and re-cross streams constantly to make our way. The water is very cold for it comes from the ice melt from the mountains, and my feet are frequently numb. We camped early, as all are tired and short-tempered. Two of the men had a fistfight over something that no one can remember now. They hammered away at each other for close to an hour! Nobody won. They just got tired and quit.

August 22, 1862
Fraser River

We are at the headwaters of the Fraser River! Here, some of the water flows east, and some flows west. The trees are different too: spruce, pine, poplar and willow to the east, and cedar, hemlock, balsam and soft maple to the west. It was thought the entire journey would take two months, but close to three months have now passed and we are still in the heart of the mountains, with no end in sight. Unfortunately, we only packed food for two months. The Schuberts shot a horse for food, and gave a small amount to the Dyers. Other men killed an ox and dried thin strips of meat over a fire to preserve it. Mr. Dyer hopes not to kill his ox. Some of the men complain of sharp pains in their legs and others' gums bleed. Talbot showed me a tooth that was loose, then got all embarrassed and snapped his mouth shut. I asked him why and he said, "Because you're a girl."

"So what? You knew I was a girl long before this," I said. "*And* you still call me Harry."

"It's just different now that everyone knows," Talbot said.

This is an example of the new strangeness between us. I wish he'd stop it!

August 24, 1862

I would not have believed it had I not tasted it myself, but skunk makes fine eating. For a creature that stinks so horribly, it sure tastes wonderful.

André Cardinal showed us how to cook it, and most of us had a taste. But a bite, unfortunately, was not enough to fill me. Our guide also told us the Indians boiled and ate the black moss that hangs from the trees, mixed with lichen from the cedars. Mrs. Schubert boiled some up. It looked absolutely disgusting and tasted dreadful, but we ate it anyway. Then Joe very kindly brought us some huckleberries he had picked.

It is Sunday but we continued our journey today — the first Sunday we have travelled since we set out — as our food is so low we had to press on or starve. I worry for Mrs. Schubert. Despite the meat from the horse they killed, she seems very tired. I took the two eldest children to walk with me.

August 25, 1862

All are gloomy of thought tonight. But there is no going back now.

August 26, 1862

A night and day as I'd never want to repeat. We camped on the steep side of the mountain and I lay awake all night, fearful of rolling down. Then we had to cross a narrow ledge, barely a foot broad, covered with loose slate and once again a sheer drop on one side. The men packed the goods across on their own backs rather than risk the animals. They helped Mrs. Schubert and the children over, and Talbot went to help me, but I pulled my arm away from his hand. It makes me mad he thinks I need help just because I'm a girl. But as soon as I stepped out on that ledge I wished I'd not been so quick to push him away! My heart pounded so loud I was sure the men could hear, but I inched my way across and collapsed on the other side until my heart stilled. Mama was right. I am far too stubborn.

August 27, 1862
Tête Jaune Cache

We lost a horse today. It was so tired of walking it just gave up and died. I know exactly how it feels.

We arrived at Tête Jaune Cache around four in the afternoon. The men are celebrating our arrival with huckleberry wine provided by a camp of Shuswap Indians we came upon. I don't know why they are celebrating. There is no sign of a trail or road here to Cariboo as the men at Fort Edmonton said there would be. If I pass by that fort again, I swear I will go in and give them a piece of my mind.

I'm sitting some ways off with Mrs. Schubert and the children, listening to the toasts and cheers, feeling very annoyed that I'm not in the thick of things. This being a girl is a confounded nuisance. But it does give me time to write in you, dear diary.

August 28, 1862

There is good pasturage here for the stock and we are able to trade with the Indians for salmon and berry cakes, so we are staying a few days to rest. Berry cakes are made by mashing berries to a pulp, and spreading the pulp on sticks to dry — very tasty. I traded my thread and needle for some as my clothes are so tattered, no amount of sewing will mend them anyway.

The men have decided to split up to help with the food problem. One party will build rafts and go down the Fraser River — a dangerous route, the Indians tell us — while a second party will go overland with the animals to the Thompson River — a longer route, but hopefully, safer. It is up to each person which route they want to take. Talbot and Mr. Dyer plan to go the Fraser Route. The Schuberts, the Thompson River Route. Joe and Henry have not yet decided. (They have not, dear diary, entirely made up their quarrel, so neither wants to give in to what the other wants.)

Mrs. Schubert says I should continue with her, but the aspens are turning golden, and the ground is white with frost in the mornings, and I feel time pushing at my back. I need to get to the gold fields as soon as possible for I *have* to find Father before the snows come. I cannot live an entire winter out west alone. And when summer comes Mrs. Owen will take Luella and William away.

I just don't know which way to go. The Fraser route scares me, but is faster; the Thompson route is safer. My brain is in a burning turmoil. Either way I choose to go will break my heart, as it means saying goodbye to someone.

August 29, 1862

I have decided on the Fraser River route. I expect some people — I mean John and Thomas Drummond — won't like my decision, so one part of me wants to wait until morning to tell Mr. McMicking, but another part says, "Do it now. Get it over with." That part won. I'll tell Mr. McMicking now.

Night

There were some protests against my going on the Fraser route — and as I expected, mostly from John and his brother! They make me so angry. They said I'd hold everyone back.

Henry spoke up and said that he and Joe would be willing to watch out for me. (They finally decided on the Fraser River.) Henry said I'd proven myself a good traveller and I'd grumbled less than some on the journey — and he looked right at Thomas Drummond! I thought Thomas would go for him, but Joe wandered over beside Henry, and that ended that. Then Mr. Dyer and Talbot said I'd be welcome with them also.

John said, "It's not proper, her being a girl."

Henry said, the way he saw it, out here, proper be damned, "Beg your pardon, Mrs. Schubert."

Whether I am a girl or not, no longer matters. We all just wanted to get to Cariboo without starving! It looks like I'm going down the Fraser River. I'm scared to death!

August 30, 1862

Today is my birthday. I'm thirteen years old. Kept it to myself.

September 1, 1862, morning

Several rafts have been built over the last few days. Mr. Sellar tells me they are 45 feet long and 20 feet broad. My job was to chink the cracks in the rafts with small poles so the cattle would not get their feet caught. "You better do a good job on those," John said.

I ignored him, but worked doubly hard to prove my worth to the men. There are double oarlocks on each end of the raft, so if the rafts break apart the men will still be able to steer them. Most of the animals will go with the Thompson River party, but we killed some and dried the meat to take with us. (I am heartily sick of dried meat!) A couple of rafts will carry a few oxen, mules and horses in case we need to slaughter them too.

Canoes were also made, hollowed out of large cottonwood logs. Some men stitched together hides and stretched them over a frame and made a watertight conveyance in that fashion, though it looks to me like it could tip easily. I'll stick to the larger rafts!

Now it is time to leave. I am to be on a raft with Joe, Henry, Mr. Dyer and Talbot, among others — two of those others unfortunately being John and Thomas Drummond! It seems God is testing me!

My heart is in my throat at the thought of our river journey, but I keep reminding myself that I will soon be in Cariboo and with Father.

September 2, 1862

If only the whole journey had been this easy! No trail cutting, no swamps, no bridge making or walking. As we pushed off from shore yesterday I had one moment of panic when I saw the Indians watch us go and sadly shake their heads. One shouted something, but I couldn't make out his words, so asked Talbot. At first he wouldn't tell me, but I wheedled it out of him — then wished I hadn't. "Poor white men no more," is what the Indian said. I wanted to get off the raft right then and there, because if anyone would know the river it would be the Indians! But as we continue on without mishap, my fears have settled down.

The worst part was saying goodbye to the Thompson River Route party. We came all this way together, and not one life lost, and now we're split up. My heart was very heavy to leave the Schuberts. Sometimes it seems like all I do is say goodbye to people — to Father when he left for Cariboo, to Mama when she died, to William. I never did say goodbye to Luella.

September 3, 1862

It rains constantly. I am soaked through, but then I don't believe I've been dry more than a couple days the entire journey anyway, so I guess it doesn't matter! We tried to light a fire on the raft to warm some water for the meagre bit of tea we have left, but just as a flame caught, a wave broke over and put it out. Our tea will have to wait until we land for nightfall. At least I get to rest and catch up with my diary writing, though I worry that I am using a lot of pages. I will write smaller. I recall Mama writing a letter one day and when she ran out of paper, she turned it sideways and wrote over her own writing in a slightly larger hand. I will do that if necessary.

Talbot is talking to Joe. I wish he wouldn't. It is Joe's turn to watch the river for gravel bars and he has trouble doing more than one thing at once. It is easy for the raft to catch up on the bars and then we have a time of it getting free. Most of the others are napping. It is hard to sleep at night, the ground onshore being cold and wet and hard. Every night I thank Mrs. Sinclair for giving me the buffalo skin as I spread it between me and the ground. I guard it with my life!

It has kept out

Later

Sorry I left so abruptly, dear diary, but it was as I feared. Joe was talking with Talbot and missed seeing the gravel bar. "You don't use the few brains the Lord gave you, you daft ox," Henry yelled. I could see Joe's mind turning over and over, but all he could come up with was, "Don't call me an ox, you . . . you mule."

Talbot told me he feels bad for distracting Joe and I told him he should! It took hours to get off the gravel bar, which didn't help anyone's temper, especially with Thomas grumbling at Joe every darn minute.

September 4, 1862

I can't stop crying. A tragedy has struck us! Early today the canoe with Mr. Warren, Mr. Robertson and Mr. Douglas overtook us on the river. We waved gaily at each other. A couple of hours later we came upon a small gravel bar mid-river and there sat Mr. Warren and Mr. Douglas, but Mr. Robertson was nowhere to be seen! We rescued them and they told us that they'd hit rapids and overturned. The canoes run the rapids considerably faster than we do on our rafts, and overturn easily as well. Mr. Robertson had struck out for shore with the idea he'd get help, while the others clung to the canoe. Eventually they made their way to a gravel bar, but there was no sign of Mr. Robertson. We searched the shores for hours, but could not find him, so presume he is drowned. He was a very nice man, Mr. Robertson, not one of those that grumbled.

Moments later

John just walked by and said. "Crying, just like a girl."

"But I AM a girl," I yelled at him. Then I called him a word that girls aren't supposed to know. Joe and Talbot's mouths nearly dropped to the ground, though I thought I saw Mr. Dyer smile. "Begging your pardon," I said.

When he finally got his mouth closed, Talbot said to not mind John, as we'll soon be at the gold fields and well away from him. But I look at Talbot, Mr. Dyer, Joe, Henry and the others on the raft, and I wonder if they will arrive safely at Cariboo — and will I?

September 5, 1862

We are all unwell with a bowel complaint. And a raft is not the best place for that! I fear we've eaten bad meat.

September 6, 1862

Most of the men sleep, so I am taking advantage of the quiet to write in you, dear diary. It is beautiful country that slides past us. I don't know why people call rock grey. It is really made up of wondrous colours: warm brown, pink, black. Today lowering clouds have softened the stark ridges and swallowed the uppermost spires of evergreens. We pass tree-filled gullies and thickets that

Later

Another mishap, though no lives were lost in this one. As I was writing I heard a tremendous roar of water over rock! The men poling the raft shouted to wake those who were sleeping. Everyone rushed to the oars to make our way to shore, but then over the water's thunder I heard Talbot shout, "Man overboard!"

I whipped around and saw Joe plunging into the water. At first I thought it was he fallen over, but soon realized it was Henry! I saw Joe's head go down, up, then down again, and finally he surfaced with Henry in his grasp. They bobbed towards the rapids, but no one could help as everyone strained at the oars to bring the raft ashore. Without thinking I grabbed a knife and slashed the rope holding the rail together, wrestled the pole free and held it out to Joe. Just then Talbot and Mr. Dyer came up and grabbed the pole also and we were able to pull Joe in. He hoisted Henry onto the raft.

Once Henry had coughed up what looked like a bucket of river water, he began to feel better.

Evening
Shore of the Fraser River

Joe is quite the hero, though a bewildered one. Every time he passes him, Henry, much recovered, thumps Joe on the back. Joe grins widely. They're best of friends again. I told Joe he was very brave to jump into the river and gave him a kiss on the cheek. He turned beet red, then said, "Of course I jumped in, it was Henry." I guess that says it all. Mr. Dyer said I was very quick-thinking. I was just glad that for once my brain was not in a burning turmoil.

I am sitting onshore while the men discuss how to proceed. We have come to a place in the river where it narrows drastically in a canyon and is full of rapids. The water rushes and swirls in a circle at one spot. A whirlpool, it is called.

It is decided that there is nothing for it but to try to take the rafts through the rapids and whirlpool.

Either that or we starve where we are. Some are to take provisions to lighten the raft and walk around the rapids, including myself and Talbot, as it is considered safer for the youngsters. Talbot's face has been set in a scowl all morning at being lumped together with me as a "youngster" and needing to be kept safe. Joe and Henry will go on the raft, Joe because his strength is needed, and Henry because he has a calm head.

September 7, 1862

Back on the raft. My heart was in my throat watching the men take the raft through the rapids yesterday. Once the current got hold of it, the raft swept rapidly into the narrow canyon. Water broke against rocks all around it in huge sprays of white foam. At one point the raft went underwater, and we all groaned with dismay, but it resurfaced, all the men safe. They rounded the sharp bend towards the whirlpool and we lost sight of them, but a few minutes later we heard a loud cheer above the water's roar, so knew they had made it safely.

September 8, 1862, evening
Fort George

We have arrived at Fort George, though it is a sad arrival. Mr. Pattison died. Dr. Stevenson said it was diphtheria and nothing could be done. He was ill with a sore throat when we started down the Fraser, and was shipwrecked for two days with no provisions or shelter when their canoe broke up in the rapids. We also hear of another canoeist drowned, though I did not know him very well.

A couple of the men found a field of potatoes and helped themselves to a few. Mr. Hunniford protested that it was stealing, but then shrugged. We've all changed out here. We had the potatoes with fish for supper and relished both!

September 9, 1862
Fraser River — Again!

We are again on the raft, with Indian guides to take us to Quesnellemouth. We soon came upon rapids and as before, I and Talbot and many others walked around them, but the raft made it through safely. As Joe recounted the exciting ride on the raft through the rough water, Talbot turned pea green with envy at missing such an adventure, and stomped off to be on his own.

John accidentally dropped one of Thomas's packs into the river when we unloaded the raft. Thomas said he was good for nothing and clipped him on the side of the head. John fell to the ground and Thomas went to hit him again, when Mr. Dyer stepped forward and said, "That isn't called for. It was an accident."

John got to his feet and shot a murderous look at Thomas. It left us all upset. They are really disagreeable people.

We're camped tonight near a party of Chinamen. I've never seen a Chinaman before and find them quite fascinating with their pigtails and yellow skin, and the chopsticks they use to eat with rather than fork and knife. The Chinamen are working sand and gravel bars for gold. I wanted to ask them if they knew Father, but Mr. Dyer said it was not seemly for me to talk to them. Confound seemly!

September 11, 1862
Quesnellemouth

We are at the mouth of the Quesnel River! In Cariboo! But all are low in spirits. It's a rude place this; the buildings are slapped together. Two stores have provisions, though they are quite dear. There is an eating house, Indians' huts and a gambling tent. They'll find us poor customers.

Most of the men ate their meal off a table for the first time in nearly four months, but I did not have the money to pay for a bought meal — bacon and beans cost $2.50! I made my meal of dried meat and a biscuit before my own small fire. I feel at times like a hen, scratching, scratching for my living.

What has caused the men's low spirits is the fact that there are miners here — all returning empty-handed from the gold fields! Where are the riches? Now I am afraid that I will have missed Father. That like these miners, he might have left Cariboo. I never thought of this before. I leapt before I looked! What if he became disillusioned and decided to return while I came west! I went quickly among the miners, giving Father's name, but none had heard of him. Talbot told me it was to be expected, as there were thousands of miners working the gold fields. I know he meant it to comfort me, but it only made me realize the foolhardiness of my journey. As Mama would say — like finding a needle in a haystack. I should never have come.

September 12, 1862

More rafts have arrived. We hear of the death of two more canoeists, one very eerie indeed. Mr. Carpenter left a note on shore that others found after he had already left in a canoe. It said: *Arrived this day at the canyon at 10 a.m. and drowned running the canoe down. God keep my poor wife.*

Joe was quite bug-eyed to know how Mr. Carpenter knew he would die. Talbot told him he didn't know for sure, he probably just had a feeling in his gut. Then Talbot got quite red. "Stomach, I mean," he said quickly.

"I do know what a gut is," I told him. Joe was very quiet for a while, then clutched his stomach. I asked if he was unwell, and he said he was just seeing if he had a feeling in his gut that he was going to die. He looked so scared, I reassured him he was going to live a long, long time. Henry was quite disgusted and told him not to be so daft. Even though they're friends again, Joe and Henry still bicker.

Late afternoon

After a day of talk, talk and more talk, most of the men have decided they are tired of travelling and will continue to the coast and Victoria for the winter, rather than the gold fields. Mr. McMicking complained that now that he has lugged his miner's tools all the way over the mountains, they are the only things he does not need.

I am like Joe today, clutching my stomach to find a feeling to tell me what to do, but there was no help there. I cannot afford the time, and I have no money to go to Victoria. My brain is in a burning turmoil. I need to go to the gold fields, but I'm scared. This is a rough place. We hear of terrible things and it's hard to tell what's true and what are tall tales. I heard one story — told three different ways, each one more dramatic than the one before — of a murder of a miner for his gold. Talbot said one of the Wattie brothers and Mr. Fortune plan to go on to the gold fields to take a look before winter settles in. I will ask to go with them.

Late

Talbot has been arguing with me most of the evening. He does not think I should go, but I told him I didn't travel for months over mountains and rivers to get within 60 miles of my goal and not finish my task. Joe and Henry sat with us, smoking their pipes, but saying nothing.

"Why don't you and your father come with me?"
I asked Talbot.

Talbot shook his head. "Father's illness took a
great deal out of him. He wouldn't survive the winter out here."

I immediately felt ashamed I'd asked, because it
was more for me than him I wanted him to come.
I also know Talbot is bursting to go, yet feels his
duty to his father.

I asked Henry and Joe whether they weren't
eager to see the gold fields. But Henry said they
would go to Victoria for the winter, too. They need
provisions and a rest. Henry joked that the gold
would still be here when they came back next
spring.

"But don't you want to start finding your riches
now?" I asked.

John was suddenly there, unpleasant as usual.
"Riches? You'll still be doing laundry when I've my
pockets weighed down with gold nuggets, *Harriet*.
You might even be doing my laundry."

I told him I would never do his laundry even if it
meant a horrible death by starvation! He laughed
and moved off.

I asked Henry whether he knew what the
Drummonds were doing. He said they hadn't
decided, but that whatever they did, he wouldn't

be sorry to see the last of them.

"You bet your gumboots no one will miss them," Joe added. "Always up to scurvy tricks." (He's started to talk like the miners he has met, all grub and scurvy tricks and gumboots, much to Henry's disgust.)

Then Talbot pleaded with Henry to tell me it wasn't safe for me to go to Cariboo.

"Can't change a woman's mind once it is made up, boy," Henry said. I sat up straighter at that — a *woman*.

But then Talbot, as usual, spoiled it! "A *woman's* mind! Stubborn, that's what she is. Worse than a mule," he grumbled. How flattering to be compared to a mule!

He then told me that if I kept wearing my boy's clothes and didn't talk much, no one would know I'm a girl from my looks. I glared at him and stomped away! Honestly! I can't help it if I'm skinny and don't have my woman's figure yet. I'm half-starved from climbing over mountains!

September 13, 1862, midday

More goodbyes. There is a lump in my throat, dear diary, as I write this, as there has been all morning. Parting from Joe and Henry, Mr. Dyer, and yes, even Talbot (though I'm still mad at him) was the hardest thing I've ever done. Even harder than leaving Luella and William, but that is because I didn't have much time to think about leaving them, and I know I'll see them again, but I doubt I'll ever see Talbot and the others again. Joe gave me a huge hug and said he had a *feeling* in his gut I would find my father. "You bet your gumboots. You'll find him." I hugged him back extra hard for his *feeling*. Henry solemnly shook my hand and said. "You're a fine lass."

Even writing that makes me start crying, and I don't want Mr. Wattie or Mr. Fortune to see me weeping like a baby! I told them I'd be no trouble. But my heart is so sore.

I will tell of leaving Talbot, because that certainly will dry my tears! Talbot stood nearby all the time I said my goodbyes, digging his toes into the dirt. When it came his turn, he said. "I didn't mean you don't look like a girl, I only meant, you look like a boy in boy's clothes. But I know you are a girl, even though you don't exactly look like one . . . "

Henry groaned, and the men standing around snickered, making me all embarrassed and mad and sharp-tongued. "Oh, do be quiet!" I snarled and left without saying goodbye to him. Now I feel bad about that.

Evening

My legs feel about to drop off! The walking is difficult, as the trail is much-travelled and muddy. It sucks at my feet, and my new boots don't help. My old boots cramped my toes — I guess I've grown — and my moccasins were worn to shreds, so I had to part with the last of my money for a second-hand pair of boots that were dirt cheap. They are iron heeled with inch-thick soles full of round-headed nails that dig into my feet. No wonder they were so cheap!

We barely made 15 miles today on our way to Cottonwood Wayouse. I had thought I was done with crawling over fallen trees, slipping on loose rock on steep slopes, and wading through swamps, but here I am at it again.

We have an ox with us to carry our packs, mine mostly being made up of provisions and cooking utensils. I have no clothes left but the ones I wear, as the last of my laundry money went for bacon, beans and flour. I won't even allow myself to think about what will happen if I don't find Father. No matter how destitute I become, I swear I will not do laundry for John!

The trees are dripping icy rainwater down my neck. You'd think I'd be used to the wet by now after months of travelling, but it's still uncomfortable. I am very lonely, dear diary. Mr. Wattie and Mr. Fortune are kind, but they're not Talbot or Joe or the Schuberts. I had hoped to have news of the Schuberts before leaving, but nothing has been heard. I think of the men drowned in the rapids, and hope she and the children are safe.

September 14, 1862
Cottonwood Wayhouse

Such a sight I never have seen before, nor will ever likely again. We have passed pack trains of mules, but this was a pack train of camels! Yes, camels! What strange looking animals with their long noses and humped backs. And the stink! Our ox shied away from them, tossing its head and acting much disturbed until Mr. Fortune led him off the trail while the animals passed. The camels were originally brought from Russia to the United States when gold was discovered in California, one packer told us, and then came up here. The men with them said a camel can carry upwards of 700 lbs. and does not need the feed or water that oxen do, but it bites and kicks and scares mules! Then they hoisted me up on one! Very unlike riding a horse and I soon scrambled down.

September 15, 1862

Talbot is here! Shortly after we set off this morning from Cottonwood Wayhouse, there was a great commotion behind us, and a voice shouted, "Harry! Harry!" It was Talbot.

"You'll never sneak up on anyone," I told him.

It seems Mr. Dyer couldn't stand Talbot's long face, and told him to go see the gold fields for himself, then meet him in Victoria for the winter — though I did not hear Talbot's entire story as I was trying to clean myself off! I was so surprised to see him that my foot caught in one of those infernal roots on the trail and I tumbled face first into a mud pool. Talbot collapsed laughing when he saw me covered from head to foot in the stinking stuff, but at least he didn't rush to my rescue like I was a girl or something. As I struggled to free myself, I slipped backwards and fell again. Now that I think of it, how could Talbot sit there laughing and not help me up!

September 16, 1862

The men thought I was sleeping and were talking amongst themselves. I heard Talbot tell them that he also came because the Drummonds had decided to go directly to Cariboo to find gold rather than winter in Victoria, and Talbot wanted to stake his claim, too, fearing there would be none left next spring. I didn't like hearing that John and Thomas were around.

We shared a fire with a returning miner last night. He told us that many of the creeks are yielding gold: Keithly, Antler, Harvey, Snowshoe and Grouse were some of them — so many! I'm not sure how I will ever find Father. The miner said he ran out of supplies and money before he could find his riches, like so many others, so he was forced to pack out. Then he told us about Williams Creek, named for William "Dutch Bill" Dietz, who made a gold find there. And how a man named Billy Barker located an even bigger find below the Black Jack Canyon. Some people take out anywhere from $40.00 to $300.00! A day!

September 17, 1862

We passed a group of Indian packers. Even the women carry heavy loads of food and tools on their backs, more than we carry. We left our ox with a herd of cattle and now carry our provisions ourselves. The men each carry 40 lbs. of flour, beans, rice, bacon, tea, salt and sugar, a tarp, bedroll, axe, pick, shovel, gold pan and firearms. My pack is considerably lighter as I don't carry miners' tools, and little food and no firearms.

September 18, 1862

We are in the gold fields! But now that we're actually *here*, I have no idea where to go.

September 19, 1862
Williams Creek — Cariboo!

We are at Williams Creek. Talbot and I decided to stick with Mr. Wattie and Mr. Fortune, who wanted to come here. Gold fever has struck them all hard. Talbot's brain is completely addled. He bought a gold pan from a miner, paying a ridiculously high price for it, and immediately stuck it into the creek. A man came running, gun in hand, and shouted at him that it was his claim and to clear off. (I have, dear diary, used much nicer words than the man really said.)

Evening

How on earth will I ever find Father here? Never have I seen such a sight as Williams Creek! Every foot of ground is staked. Men scurry about everywhere. They seem somewhat leery of newcomers. Mr. Wattie carried his rifle in plain view today. Chinamen scratch around on old gravel bars that have already been worked. All day long we heard the sounds of saws and axes, men's shouts, the creak of what the miners call Cornish wheels, the splash of water, the ringing strike of metal pick on stone, and trees falling. Even as we sit here before our evening fire, the din continues. As I look out, I see fires lining the creek, lanterns carried by shadowy figures, illuminating men still bent over their shafts. We're told they work around the clock to get the gold out.

The hillsides are stripped bare of trees, and the land has great cracks running through it. Shanties and tents — with great dumps of dirt and gravel behind — and rockers, sluices, and windlasses line the creek. And the talk of gold is everywhere! I swear it is part of the air we breathe.

September 20, 1862

You won't believe this, dear diary, but I have caught gold fever! All along I thought it foolish that men left home and family — that Father left *us!* — to seek gold. But I begin to understand why, now!

A miner showed us around his claim. He has a

partner, but he'd gone to Richfield, a few miles away, for provisions. While it is true some of the men here are secretive and unwelcoming, others are friendly, and once they know we do not mean to steal their gold, proudly show off their stakes.

The miner showed us how they diverted the stream with sluices to the side of the creek to leave the gravel exposed. Then he took a pan and handed it to me, and dumped a shovelful of dirt and gravel into the pan. He told me to lower it into the water and move it in circles. At first it felt quite clumsy, but I soon got the rhythm of the motion. I broke up the gravel with my fingers and tossed away the larger stones. On my third shovelful, the miner leaned over the pan and pointed at a speck of yellow. "You got some colour there," he said.

"You mean — gold?" I asked.

"Yup."

And that was all it took. My heart pounded with excitement.

Talbot turned pea green that I was the one who first touched gold.

I wanted to keep panning, but had to give the pan back.

The man then showed us a rocker and a wooden cradle into which gravel and dirt are shovelled. Water is added from the diverted stream and as the

cradle is rocked, the gold collects on the riffles —
ridges on the bottom of the cradle — while the dirt
washes through. He offered me a job for a few days
rocking the cradle until his partner returned. I des-
perately need the money, but the nights are cold
and shorter now and I must find Father before winter sets in, so refused. Talbot refused, too. He wants
his own claim. Before I left I asked the miner if he
knew Father, but he didn't. He did tell us that he
used to be a clerk in a printing office in San Francisco.

September 21, 1862

I am tired and hungry and desperate-feeling.
Talbot, though, is in high spirits, excited by all he
sees. It is very vexing.

We went down the creek below the canyon. Here
the men dig deep shafts into the creek bed. We got
a closer look at the huge Cornish wheels. They look
similar to our water wheel at the mill at home, and
are used to drive pumps to remove water from the
shafts. Even when the creeks freeze up, the shafts
can still be worked in the winter, though we hear
that only a hardy few miners stay on their claims, as
most of the men head south to Victoria or New
Westminster. We came upon two men who had

been digging for two months without success, yet at the claim next to them, the men are taking gold out of the earth at a fierce rate. That is how it is out here.

I watched as one man was lowered in a bucket into the shaft by a windlass. The rope is wrapped around a large wooden pole with a handle that is built over the shaft. Another man turns the handle to raise or lower the bucket. At times the men use ladders to go into the shafts. I wonder that they can keep digging day after day and find nothing. I would soon be disheartened.

I asked the miners if they knew Father. They thought for a bit, discussed it among themselves, then agreed they didn't know him. I immediately burst into tears, something I know a boy would not do! One of the men was quite stricken and patted my shoulder. "Try Richfield, boy," he said. "If he's in this area, they'd know him there at the mining office."

The miners offered Mr. Wattie and Mr. Fortune a share of their stake if they would provide food for them for two weeks, as they were out of provisions and their claim had not yet made them any money to buy more. But Mr. Wattie and Mr. Fortune said they were going to Victoria to winter and were merely here a short while to look things over.

We also came across a miner working his claim alone, though I don't think it is *his* claim. I think it is *HER* claim. I think this miner was really a woman! Most miners here have beards, but this one was clean-shaven with no hint of even a single whisker on the chin. He (or she) said very little, but did have a high-pitched voice when speaking. As we left, I turned back to stare once more, and the miner suddenly winked.

September 24, 1862
Richfield

Mr. Wattie and Mr. Fortune wanted to see Richfield. The settlement is ringed by low mountains, and borders Williams Creek. Higher up, the slopes are covered with trees and it should be a pretty place, but it isn't! In fact, it is quite possibly the worst looking place I've ever seen. The land around the town is barren, all the trees having been chopped down willy-nilly, leaving ugly stumps sticking out. Piles of discarded trash and dirt are everywhere. Tents and rough wooden shanties line the creek into the town. We smelled the settlement before we saw it — wood smoke, cut pine, frying bacon and — I swear — beans.

There are several stores here to provision miners

(with more being built), eating places, a hotel, a log jail, a bank and a church (Roman Catholic) and of course, gambling houses and saloons. Mr. Wattie and Mr. Fortune told Talbot and me to go look around while they went into a saloon. Talbot's nose was out of joint for a while as he thought himself quite old enough for a saloon. He was so busy ranting about that, he didn't look where he was going and stepped in a fresh pile of mule droppings. That made him even more vexed.

Father was never one for drink — a bad habit, Mama said, and as she hated bad habits and didn't let us have any, Father didn't drink. We did have other bad habits though, ones I am now sorry I taxed her with. Like my stubbornness, which she didn't have much success ridding me of, or Father's restless feet. Dear diary, if I could have Mama back, I'd work awful hard at ridding myself of my bad habit of being stubborn. But I guess that's closing-the-barn-door-after-the-horse-has-left wishing.

We wandered about, a pack of dogs barking and nipping at our heels, and I kept having a niggling feeling that something was missing. Then I realized what it was — there wasn't a school. But then, there weren't any children.

I carefully examined every man we passed. They all have whiskers, and I realized that if Father has grown a beard I might pass right by him. And with myself dressed as a boy, he might pass right by me! One man yelled at me, "What are you staring at, boy?" I quickly stammered, "Nothing," and looked away.

Then I saw the mining office. I dragged Talbot in there and asked the clerk if George Palmer had staked a claim. The clerk asked when Father arrived at Cariboo. I told him I didn't know. My answer vexed him, as he sighed deeply, flipped through a book, barely looking, and said he had no record of any George Palmer. I wanted to ask him to look again, but he was so impatient, I didn't dare.

Here is a sketch of Richfield.

September 25, 1862

I thought I saw John and Thomas Drummond today, but I lost sight of them quickly. Talbot said it is unlikely we'd run into them here, as Cariboo is a really big place, and there are thousands of miners around. I want to believe he's right, but I feel very unsettled.

September 26, 1862

It has turned quite cold. Still no sign of Father. No one I've asked knows his name.

September 27, 1862

The ground is white with snow and it swirls about us still. Seeing it terrifies me. Mr. Wattie, Mr. Fortune and Talbot are to leave today for the coast. They want to go before the snow makes their journey impossible. They urged me to go with them, as they said they didn't feel right leaving me on my own. For a while there I thought the three of them were going to *make* me go with them, but I managed to hold out. It wasn't easy. "Harry," Talbot said. "This is just the first bad weather. Winter will be here soon. Come to Victoria, and in the spring we'll come back and find your father. I promise." But I told him that

I had a gut feeling that Father was nearby and that if I waited until spring, he might be gone, and Mrs. Owen would take Luella and William away and I would never see them again! I smiled as cheerily as I could and told him I'd be fine. I don't think he believed me. *I* don't believe me. But I have no choice.

They are ready to leave now. I must say goodbye.

Evening

Talbot has stayed! "Can't have you finding all the gold," he said. "I'd never hear the end of it."

I could have hugged him for staying — I hate to admit it, but it scared me nearly to death, thinking of being on my own. Instead I said, "Whatever suits you." And immediately felt bad for saying that so offhandedly, because he looked a bit hurt. He sent a message to his father with Mr. Wattie, who is much relieved that at least I won't be on my own.

We're camped outside of Richfield. I try to keep my mind off the coming winter, but it's hard when my feet feel like blocks of ice and my fingers are too numb to hold the pen anymore!

September 28, 1862

Icy rain dripped on me all night long, Talbot's tent being next to useless. I'm so tired this morning

I can barely see the words I write. It doesn't help that I have no tea or biscuits for breakfast. I'm very low today. I think I expected Father to be right here to greet me when I arrived, not me having to hunt and hunt for him.

Now I've gone making myself feel sorry, and thinking about Mama, William and Luella, Henry and Joe and the Schuberts. It's like everyone I meet leaves a little splinter in me when they part, and it keeps jabbing me, making me hurt.

Talbot asked why I was sniffing. I told him it was the cold. I'll have to take Mama's watch into town and see if I can buy provisions. I wanted to yell at Talbot for spending all his money on the gold pan, but I can't. It's my fault he's even here.

September 29, 1862

I awoke this morning with four walls around me for the first time in close to five months, though I share my room with a horse and two mules. Still, I took a moment to enjoy those walls, even with the cracks between the boards letting in the cold! Talbot would not stay here, despite my urging, saying it wasn't proper now that we were in town. "Proper be hanged," I said, but he returned alone to our camp.

I have a job! At a saloon! Mama, and I suspect even Father, would not approve, but it was either this job or starve. Yesterday I was determinedly making my way down the main street, trying to decide where to try to sell Mama's watch, when a saloon door crashed open and a man sailed out and landed at my feet. Another man followed, though this one stomped down the steps rather than flew, and gave the other a kick in the side. The first man didn't move, just lolled there with his mouth hanging slack and his eyes rolled back in his head.

"Well, that's done it," the second man said.

"Done what?" I asked, though I was a bit nervous, as he looked so mad.

"He's my cook, but look, he's useless. Drunk as a skunk," the man said. "Got into my liquor, and me with a room full of hungry men wanting breakfast."

I have no idea, dear diary, why I did this, but I told him I could make biscuits.

The man eyed me for such a long time I started to get antsy. "Tell you what," he said. "I'll take you on this morning because I'm desperate. But it's not a regular job, you understand?"

And next thing I knew I was in the kitchen mixing flour and water, brewing coffee and frying up potatoes and slivers of meat (to make it go further).

106

It just about killed me cooking all that food, and knowing none of it was for me.

After two hours the men cleared out and the owner came into the kitchen. "I don't know how you did it, boy, but you fed them all, and more importantly, they left without grumbling."

I think he saw me swaying on my feet because he pulled out a chair and stuck me on it, and banged the skillet with the burnt remains of potatoes and meat and two biscuits in front of me. "Get that into you." Then he offered me the job of cooking breakfast every morning.

He asked about my family, so I told him about Mama dying, my brother and sister at the Red River Settlement, and me looking for Father. I didn't let on that I was a girl, but I did tell him Father's name.

"Never heard of him," he said. "But this isn't a bad place for you to stop for a while. Everybody in the area comes in here at some time or other."

I told him Father doesn't drink, but he said it didn't matter, since Father might still come in for a meal or something.

I wasn't sure if he meant it, or whether he was just desperate for someone to cook breakfast. I eyed the last biscuit, feeling a little hollow spot that needed filling, but thought it rude to eat while he was talking, so left it on the plate. I could have it when he went.

He said I could stay in the shed out back. "There's a couple mules there, and whatever other animal people want to board for the night. You can have the care of them, too."

I asked if that included camels. They stink so bad, I doubt I could sleep with them. He said he wouldn't have camels because they stir up the mules, and he picked up the remaining biscuit and nibbled at it.

My chores are: cook breakfast, sweep the saloon floor, empty the spittoons (I'm not looking forward to that!) haul water and wood, shovel the droppings from in front of the door and tend the mules. In return I get the shed to sleep in, breakfast and dinner. He offered me a wage of fifty cents a day. I asked for more than that and we settled on a dollar. I had to point out to him that I didn't eat much, though I would have liked that biscuit he ate! His name is Mr. Mallard (like the duck!) and he's yelling right now that it's 4:30 a.m. and when was I planning to start the biscuits.

October 1, 1862

I can see why Mr. Mallard's cook took to drink! Mr. Mallard yells and shouts all the day long! Yet when one of the men aimed a kick at me for moving the spittoon (how was I to know they had the spitting distance measured exactly!), Mr. Mallard grabbed the man by the back of his coat and hustled him out the door and told him not to come back. Then he himself yelled at me for moving the spittoon.

I asked every single person I saw, but nobody has heard of Father.

I'm so tired tonight I can't see straight to write any more. Which is probably a good thing, as the account book is nearly full.

October 2, 1862

Too tired to write. Too tired to hunt for Father.

October 3, 1862

Some goods arrived at the saloon today wrapped in paper. I asked Mr. Mallard if I could have the wrapping. "You want my paper *and* to be paid?" he asked. I just stared at him until he told me to take the paper. Now I have some extra for writing and a sketch or two.

The saloon is a good size. There is a long bar like a high table along one wall. Mr. Mallard stands behind it and guards the bottles of liquor behind him. There are eight regular sized tables crammed into the remaining room, with a stove in the middle for heat. At the back of the saloon are three rooms, one for Mr. Mallard, another with four cots crammed into it for paying guests, and another where men who are nearly broke can pay less to sleep on the floor. The men in these rooms change constantly. "Always someone leaving," Mr. Mallard told me. "But there's new ones with a spark in their eyes arriving every day to replace them."

It is quite ripe in these rooms as most of the men, and I must admit, myself, are in sore need of a bath! You can tell if someone's struck it rich because they stay at the fancy French hotel rather than the saloon.

Attached to the back of the saloon, like an afterthought, is the kitchen, with a stove, a table on which to mix biscuits and slice bacon, and shelves to hold stacks of plates and cups, and very little space for me to move about without knocking my hips or knees on something.

And then there's Old Jackson. No one knows where he came from and some say he was just here when the town went up. He has a permanent cot in the back room and breakfasts here every morning, and the rest of the day he sits and drinks whiskey. All that drink, you'd think he'd be mean, but he has the manners and speech of a gentleman and doesn't use the spittoon. I tried to figure out how old he is, but could only narrow it down between thirty and one hundred years. One rumour is that he's a bank robber from New York City and is running from the law. I studied Old Jackson pretty closely on hearing that. He certainly doesn't look like a bank robber to me. Outlaws should have beady eyes, a black scowl and shifty ways. Another rumour is that Old Jackson has a hidden claim and that he's actually very rich and could stay at the French hotel if he wanted.

One miner asked if Mr. Mallard would bring in dancing girls. He was from California and told us how the saloons down there had pretty girls that the men would pay for a dance. "But don't make them wear crinolines," he said. "I don't take to crinolines on ladies — you have to take too much on trust. You don't know what they're hiding."

I saw Mr. Mallard's eyes get that gleam in them — the same look he gets when he's studying the room where the men sleep and wondering if he can fit in yet another person. I think Mr. Mallard makes more money with his saloon than most of the miners passing through. I expect we'll have dancing girls here soon.

I keep asking, but no news of Father.

October 4, 1862 (quite late at night) or October 5 (early morning) I don't know which

I slipped away from my chores today to beg Talbot to come to the saloon. There was to be a wake for a dead miner and I figured Talbot could sneak in and eat his fill, and people would think he was there to pay his respects. He asked what he'd do if someone talked about the dead man. I told him to shake his head sorrowfully and look sombre whenever anyone spoke of the deceased, and he'd do just fine.

This was my first wake and not one I'll soon forget. I remember when Grandmother Palmer died and we all sat quietly around the casket the night before the burying. And Mama's burying was even quicker. But the dead miner was Irish and had a fair amount of money, so the men said he should have a good sending off.

The wake began quietly and soberly enough. Especially as the priest from the Roman Catholic Church was there. I spent a fair amount of time studying him, as I'd never seen a priest up close before, other than the ones at St. Anne's. The priest's rosy cheeks and clean-shaven chin sure made him stand out from the whiskered miners. And of course, his black dress, though Old Jackson says it's called a cassock. The room filled up quickly (everyone in town hearing about the free drinks, I expect) and Mr. Mallard was kept on his toes, pouring. I'd been making biscuits all day, and having found some dried apples in the storeroom, made those up into pies.

"Goes down real good with this whiskey," one man said as he shovelled more pie into his mouth. He didn't even bother to use a fork! Just reached in and grabbed a handful.

I saw Talbot hovering by the door so went over and pulled him in and shoved some biscuits into his pockets before they were all gone.

When the food was all eaten the men started to tell stories about the dead miner, and when they ran out of them, one man said, "Nothing Charlie liked better than a dance." (Charlie was the dead man.)

And someone brought out his mouth organ and another his fiddle and the men began to dance — with each other, as there weren't any women — stomping in their big boots on the wooden floors until the saloon echoed and trembled from the noise.

But the worst, and funniest thing, I must admit,

was when the man who suggested the dance pulled Charlie from the casket and dragged him all over the floor for "one last dance before the grave."

Talbot's mouth gaped open and his jaw fell even further when a glass of whiskey was pushed into his hand. He divided his gaze between the dead man dancing and the whiskey, and drained the glass. Three glasses later he was up dancing with the rest of the men.

October 5, 1862, later

I never saw the like of it! This morning most of the men were holding their heads and pushing their breakfasts back to me untouched, when a miner came into the saloon, walked up to the bar and asked Mr. Mallard for a whiskey. In the morning! That brought the men's heads up from their hands. It's uncanny, but these miners have noses like bloodhounds, scenting when gold's around. "There are only two reasons to drink whiskey in the morning," Old Jackson whispered to me. "To spend your last dollar and say goodbye to Cariboo before you return home empty-handed, or to celebrate a find."

After a moment, the man who danced with the dead man last night sidled up to the miner and gave him a friendly nod. Then he says, real careless like, "Haven't seen you in here before. You new to the area?" And the man told him he was. Which meant he wasn't going home, so the whiskey was to celebrate. Everyone was alert now, like the place was one big ear listening. The miner suddenly cottoned on to that fact, put down his glass and high-tailed it out of there. The door wasn't shut behind him when every last man, except Old Jackson, began whooping, and grabbed their hats and coats and stampeded after him.

"What about the funeral?" Mr. Mallard shouted — the dead miner's funeral was later that morning. But the men never paused. They had to follow the miner to see where he'd struck it rich.

Mr. Mallard told me to clean up and then go do something else for the day, as the place was empty and he guessed he and Old Jackson had to go to the funeral. It was as I was turning around with a stack of plates that I saw Talbot standing there. He'd seen and heard everything, and his eyes had that gold-fever shine in them. He told me he was going to find his fortune.

I'm embarrassed to say that my tongue turned quite nasty from my disappointment at his leaving. "I can't say I saw any nuggets as big as strawberries for the picking."

His face turned beet red and I knew he recalled boasting about how Cariboo had nuggets to spare. Then I remembered Mama telling me it never does any good pricking a man's pride, and she was right, because I could see right then and there that Talbot was dead set to go, if just to prove me wrong, and if something happens to him, well, there's only me to blame. Too bad I hadn't remembered that before I opened my mouth.

Mr. Mallard yelled at me for not shovelling up the mule droppings in front of the door. Seems he stepped right into them.

October 8, 1862

I feel time passing, winter closing in with every frostbitten night and fallen leaf. We had one real bad snowstorm four days back, and it's snowed off and on each day since. I remember when we set out from Fort Garry how long the day stretched into the night, and now it's the night beginning to stretch into the day.

Richfield is becoming quiet, as many of the miners leave to winter in Victoria. After the day in, day out noise around here, it seems very strange. Even the saloon is emptying. I know I should be looking for Father. I need to find him soon or I'll be stuck here for the winter! But I have asked so many people if they know him, that sometimes I cannot bring myself to ask another person and hear them say no. It is as if my brain has stopped thinking and my body is too tired to move. I keep reminding myself I walked over prairies, mountains and rivers to find him, so I better get going, but instead my hands make biscuits (I'm getting quite well-known all over town for them) and sweep and shovel and I tell myself I'll search the next day.

October 9, 1862

Snowed steadily all night. I bought myself men's wool drawers from the store with my money from the saloon. I hated parting with the money, but thought it better to get the warm clothing than suffer chills and take a fever. They're very scratchy.

October 10, 1862

I have finally taken myself in hand. At breakfast I overheard the men in the saloon say that the priest goes along the creeks throughout Cariboo, ministering to the miners. He might have seen Father! I'm trying to decide if a Methodist is supposed to talk to a Roman Catholic priest. Perhaps if I'd been more pious I would have found Father by now. I used to be in the habit of going to services, and now I'm in the habit of *not* going. A new fault of mine.

I paid to send a letter to William and Luella, though I addressed it to the Chief Factor at Fort Garry, because I was afraid Mrs. Owen might open it, see it was from me, and not tell them about it. I miss them something dreadful. I told them I was real close to finding Father, which I hope I will be by the time the letter gets to them.

Evening

I'm so excited! I finally got the nerve up to speak to the priest — his name is Father Alfred — and he was very nice. He said he would "put out some inquiries," which strikes me as much more elegant than saying, "I'll ask around." My heart is leaping with excitement.

I must remember that phrase, *put out some inquiries*. I'd like to try that out on Talbot, but of course he's not here.

October 11, 1862

I'm hiding in the shed! I've had such a shock my legs have the wobbles. I was carrying dirty plates back towards the kitchen when I heard a voice I recognized. John! I quickly ran around the curtain that separates the kitchen from the saloon, and peeked out. Sure enough, there he was with his brother! Mr. Mallard is yelling for me, but I'm afraid to come out. I'll wait a bit and hopefully John and Thomas will be gone.

Evening

Father is dead, and I have probably lost Luella and William. I can't stop crying, dear diary, my heart is so sore. I don't know what to do or what will become of me.

Very late at night

I do not think I have any more tears in me. I am at a Mrs. McManus's house, as it has been decided that this is the best place for me now that I'm back to being Harriet. I will tell you what happened, dear diary, because I don't feel like I have anyone left in the whole world now except you.

John and Thomas had not left the saloon when I went back. They saw me and told Mr. Mallard I was a girl. Mr. Mallard's eyes bulged when he heard of my deception. He was hustling me out of the saloon when we ran into the priest coming in. Father Alfred's face was grave, and right then, dear diary, I knew something bad was coming.

Father Alfred told me he had found out that Father had died on Williams Creek three days ago of mountain fever. He said no one was sure where the body was at present, but he would find out.

Father is dead and all is lost.

October 12, 1862, very early

I cannot sleep. I have a *gut feeling* that tells me Father is not really dead. I wish Joe and his gut were here, or Henry or Talbot. I have no one. I overheard the priest tell Mr. Mallard that the man who had told him about Father said Father's claim was two miles down the creek and was notable for two trees having fallen across each other to form a large X. Father Alfred also told Mr. Mallard that it was rumoured that the claim was a good paying one.

Later

I am hiding behind a tree stump up on the slope above town. The sky is lightening now and soon I will be able to see well enough to walk. I dash these few sentences off to give me courage. I am scared at my own daring, dear diary, but I need to see Father's claim for myself. I put on my old clothes and took my packs and crept away from Mrs. McManus's in the early morning hours while it was still dark, so no one would see me leave. I placed the nightgown under the blanket on Mrs. McManus's spare bed, to look like I lie there, in the hopes she will think I am still asleep. My neck pricks all of a sudden, dear diary, like it does when you feel you are being spied upon. I best leave before I lose all heart.

Late afternoon

Father is not dead! He is quite ill, but very much alive! I swear I cannot take any more of these shocks! And, dear diary, Talbot is with me! He has gone to look around Father's claim. Yes — Father's. I found it. And *him*. I have so much to tell you.

I waded through deep snow along the creek. The number of miners has thinned out, most returning south to winter, with only the miners with deep shafts that can be worked in winter, or those desperate for gold, remaining. I felt very lonely, and my neck still pricking as if I were being watched, though no one was about, so I sang a song Mama used to sing to me when I was little, "Aiken Drum." I'd just got to "and he played upon a ladle, ladle, a ladle" when suddenly a voice shouted, "And we thought Joe was a terrible singer! That's the worst wailing I've ever heard!" It was Talbot! I didn't even care if it was proper or not, I gave him a great big hug. He was looking thin and I asked if he'd been eating steady. Seems he joined up with a couple of men who promised him a share of their profits when they hit gold — *I* believe they took him because he was young and could work hard. They were digging a shaft, but it filled up with water and they never found any gold. Talbot was heading back to Richfield, when he heard my singing.

Despite the snow falling heavily, we soon found two trees that formed an X, and behind them a cabin. Talbot went in first because I was too scared of what we might find. He soon came out and told me there was a man in there, ill with fever. I was absolutely terrified to go in, but made my feet move, and there on a cot was Father — a thinner, bearded Father, thrashing about and twisting the blankets. I knelt beside him and he opened his eyes. "Harriet?" he whispered. "Am I dreaming?" I told him it was really me. Even as I write these words, I am still amazed I found him.

I had Talbot build up the fire, as it was stone cold in there, and I quickly made Father some tea. I told him everyone thought him dead. He said it was his partner, Sam Simpson, who'd died of mountain fever, and that he himself had taken ill a few days ago. He is sleeping now and I have broth cooking for when he wakes.

I didn't tell him about Mama, because I worried about his strength. That can wait. I thought perhaps we should move Father to Richfield, but Talbot says the snow is too deep and the cold might make Father worse, and we should wait a day. I know Talbot is right, but I'm so scared something will happen to Father, and I couldn't stand to lose him, not now when I've just found him.

October 12, 1862, late

I can't sleep. I'm so jittery. I listen to Father's breathing, and sometimes I think it is easier, and sometimes I think it is not. It snows heavily and steadily. Trees crack and fall beneath the weight of it and I jump at every noise. I told Talbot I heard footsteps outside, but he tells me it is nothing and to stop being a Nervous Nellie.

After I got the broth into Father and he fell asleep again, Talbot and I went and looked around the claim. There is a deep shaft, which must have taken Father and his partner a long time to dig. There is a ladder in the shaft, but Talbot lowered me down in a bucket with the windlass. I was very excited, thinking I would see lots of gold, but nothing glittered. It was just cold, damp and dark. I came back to the cabin to check on Father, though

Talbot stayed a while longer. Father woke once while Talbot was still out, and told me something, dear diary, that I do not know whether to believe or not, as the fever makes him ramble in his talk. He keeps saying he hid gold "at the cross." I don't know what he means. I'm trying to decide whether or not to tell Talbot.

October 13, 1862, early morning

We found it! We found Father's gold! I was drifting off to sleep when suddenly I figured out what Father meant by "at the cross" — the two trees that mark his claim! I woke Talbot and insisted we go immediately to find it. He wasn't too excited at first to go out in the snow and cold and dark, but when I told him we were hunting for gold he perked right up. It took us a good hour, but we dug through the snow and found a hollow beneath the root of one of the trees and there was the gold! The whole time we dug, my neck pricked, but Talbot said it was me being a Nervous Nellie again. I told him I didn't like our footprints leading from the tree back to the cabin. He said he'd hide the gold again so I wouldn't have to worry. I'm waiting for him to come back now.

October 14, 1862

What an exciting time we've had! I will write it all down so I don't forget. William will think he is reading an adventure story and will be pea green with envy that it happened to me and not him. I can say this now that everything is over, but for a while I thought all was lost!

Well, Talbot did come back, but not alone! John was with him, with a rifle pointed at the middle of Talbot's back! It seems John followed me to the claim. He was returning from the saloon's privy and saw me leaving Mrs. McManus's house. He was the one that made my neck prickle! I *knew* someone was following me. Anyway, I told him I'd show him where the gold was if he left us alone and just let us get Father safely back to town! Thankfully, Father slept through the commotion.

So, rifle pointing at my back and Talbot's, we waded through knee-deep snow to the shaft. My plan was that I would tell John the gold was at the bottom of the shaft and when John climbed down the ladder to find it, Talbot and I would pull the ladder out and leave him stranded at the bottom. I was pretty proud of myself for that plan. Un-fortunately, when we got to the shaft John told Talbot to climb down and bring up the gold. I must admit I hadn't allowed for that.

Talbot wasted a bit of time fussing with the ladder and shooting hopeful glances at me, no doubt wondering what the heck my plan was and why I wasn't putting it into action. But my brain was in its worst burning turmoil of all time! Finally there was nothing left for Talbot to do but to go back down the ladder.

After a few minutes he yelled up, "Lower the bucket and I'll put the gold in it."

John gestured to me to turn the handle of the windlass to bring the bucket up. I tried to pull up the bucket, but it was heavy going. (Talbot had weighted it down with rocks, I found out later.) I let the bucket slip back down, and told John I couldn't get it up myself. He pushed me aside and took the handle, though he too found it hard going, and was forced to lay down his rifle. I thought about grabbing it, but wasn't sure if I could shoot him if need be, and by then he'd told me to help turn the handle.

We managed a few turns, but then the bucket stuck. John let go of the handle and leaned over the shaft and yelled at Talbot to see what it was caught on.

In that moment I let go of the handle myself and it flew about and caught John dead centre in the back and he tumbled headfirst down the shaft!

I was horrified. I thought I'd killed him.

At that very moment Old Jackson and Mr. Mallard came up on snowshoes. I'm embarrassed to say, dear diary, that when they arrived, I began to sob. I couldn't even breathe, I cried so hard thinking I'd murdered John.

Talbot called up that John was out cold with a goose egg on the back of his head, but was breathing fine. He emptied the rocks and managed to get John into the bucket and Mr. Mallard and Old Jackson pulled him up

We all went into the cabin, the men dragging John, who was still out cold. When he came to, Old Jackson asked him why he'd tried to steal our gold. John said he thought if he came back with gold, it would prove to Thomas that he wasn't a good-for-nothing. Seems that the rumours of Father's claim being a rich one had flown about town, and when John saw me leave Mrs. McManus's place, he decided to follow me. Old Jackson just shook his head and told John he was taking him back to Richfield to go before Judge Begbie.

John's face paled so much to hear that, I thought he'd faint dead away again. Judge Begbie has a reputation of being harsh with those who break the law. While John pleaded with Old Jackson and Mr.

Mallard not to turn him over to Judge Begbie, I pulled Talbot outside the door. Talbot started to tell me how John had managed to grab the rope halfway down the shaft to slow his fall, and if he hadn't done that, he would be dead of a broken neck, but I wasn't really that interested. I mean, I'm glad John didn't break his neck, but I had a burning question for Talbot. Where was the gold?

"In the privy, of course," he said. "The last place anyone would look."

I told him that was perfectly disgusting. He said that everything was frozen in there. Frozen or not, dear diary, it is still disgusting.

When we got back inside, Old Jackson asked me what was I doing, upsetting everyone by stealing away in the middle of the night. I apologized and told them how badly I felt that I'd put them to so much trouble. It seems Mrs. McManus had left me to sleep through the day, thinking me grief-sticken, and only sounded the alarm in the evening when she went to wake me and found it was the night-gown sleeping and not me!

Mr. Mallard and Old Jackson said they thought Father would do better back in town, so we got him bundled up and they and Talbot pulled him back to Richfield on a makeshift toboggan. John was able to make his way back with us, though he stumbled a lot. There is a doctor here who told me that mountain fever is very dangerous, and that I'm lucky Father has survived it. He does say that Father is on the mend, but will be very weak for a long time.

So right now, dear diary, I am writing this in our room at the fancy French hotel. We are staying here for the winter until Father regains his health. The hotel is really not all that fancy. In fact, I would almost rather be back in the saloon, but I guess I won't be seeing the inside of that place for some time. I did, though, have a good bath and rinsed out my boy's clothes. Mrs. McManus gave me an old skirt of hers. I've grown so much walking over the mountains that I didn't even need to shorten it.

Talbot is anxious to see his father, so he and Old Jackson are leaving shortly to go to Victoria.

I'm very sleepy, dear diary, and I will admit this hotel bed is soft. I think I am glad to not be travelling for a while. My feet are walked out. And my hand is falling off my wrist from writing so much!

October 17, 1862

Finally, Father and I had a good talk about Mama and shared a few tears over her passing. I gave him Mama's wedding ring and watch that I'd carried all this way. I told him I'd try to break my fault of stubbornness for her, but he pointed out that perhaps it was my being stubborn that kept me going all the way over prairies and mountains to find him. He gave me back the watch for my own and said Mama would be very proud of me. That brought more tears.

I told him of Luella and William, and the Owens taking them to Toronto. It sure felt good to put that worry on someone else's shoulders. He said he'd send a letter with Talbot and Old Jackson to mail once they got to Victoria, telling the Owens they were *not* to take Luella and William away, as he would be back in the spring to get them. Father said he had sent us two other letters, but they must have arrived after I left, or gone astray.

A day of goodbyes, dear diary. Old Jackson stopped by and said he didn't turn John over to the Judge after all, but to Thomas — which we both agreed might be worse than the judge! Old Jackson then said that he didn't think he'd come back to Cariboo in the spring. He says he doesn't like to be in one place too long. I finally got the nerve to ask him where he came from and he hemmed and hawed, then finally said he used to be a bank manager in New York City — I wonder if he really *was* a bank robber! — and then he told me all about

New York City. It sounds wonderful! Talbot also came by (though he'll be back, as you'll soon discover why, dear diary) and wasn't his face a picture when he saw me in a skirt! We sat on two chairs in the hotel lobby like perfect strangers while he said his goodbyes. I asked him to send me news of the Schuberts if he could, as I often think of them. It was only when I saw him to the door that I remembered this was Talbot, my best friend, and gave him a quick hug. He grinned and said, "See you in the spring, Harry," and we weren't strangers anymore.

As promised, dear diary, I will tell you why I know Talbot will be back. It is because Father has given shares in the claim over to Talbot and Mr. Dyer for their kindness in caring for me on the journey. At the mining office I asked the clerk to check the claim registration again, as he had told me Father's name was not on it. His name *was* there, right under his partner, Sam Simpson's! I knew that clerk didn't look very hard. Then Talbot and I both had the same thought, that Henry and Joe should own a share too. The proper papers will be drawn up in Victoria once Henry and Joe are located.

Father has given me a small share of my own. He asked if I wanted to return to our old home back east once we got William and Luella back. I thought about it, but told him I liked the country out here, and would be happy to stay. He agreed, and said he had money enough to take up some land here, build a good house and start a business — he says he has had quite enough of mining!

I thought I might feel desolate when they all left, but I don't. I am with Father once again, and I know I will see Luella and William soon. It was quite an adventure seeing prairies, mountains, rushing rivers and gold dust. Mama said a woman likes to be settled, not moving about all the time, but I think I'd like to see New York City some day. I hope this wanting new adventures isn't the start of another bad habit!

Epilogue

Harriet and her father spent a peaceful winter in Richfield, along with another hundred people who didn't head south to Victoria or New Westminster. When spring came, the town was fast becoming deserted in favour of the booming new town of Barkerville. By that time Mr. Palmer had regained his health, and he and Harriet made the journey south to Victoria. In late April Mr. Palmer booked passage on a ship to get William and Luella. It would take him down the west coast, across the Isthmus of Panama by railway (the Panama Canal had yet to be built), then by ship back up the eastern coast of the United States, and overland by train and steamship to Fort Garry. Travelling "across the country" before the Canadian Pacific Railway was completed — over twenty years later — was quite involved! While her father was gone, Harriet boarded with a family in Victoria and attended St. Ann's Academy.

Spring also brought the miners back to the Cariboo — Talbot and his father, and Joe and Henry Morgan among them. They began to work the Palmer claim on Williams Creek. The claim was a good one, and produced a steady output of gold, enough for all who owned a share. Harriet received her portion, which she put into the bank in Victoria.

In the early autumn Mr. Palmer returned, and Harriet had a joyful reunion with William and Luella. The family rented a house and stayed in Victoria, Harriet and the children attending school there. Harriet spent many evenings reading from her diary about her overland journey adventures to a wide-eyed Luella and pea-green-with-envy William.

In the spring of 1864 Mr. Palmer moved the family to the Okanagan Valley in the interior of British Columbia, where he homesteaded 160 acres of land on Okanagan Lake near Trout River. He raised cattle and also built a flour mill. Three years later, Mr. Dyer and Talbot took up land adjoining the Palmers, built a ranch and opened a small trading store. With the hard work of mining proving too difficult for Mr. Dyer, and with the mine's output declining, he and Talbot left the operation to Joe and Henry.

In 1869, Talbot and Harriet were married, something their fathers expected even though the couple still sparred at just about every opportunity. Harriet took over the running of the store so Talbot could devote himself to raising cattle on the ranch. They often talked of their overland journey, Talbot jumping at every opportunity to remind Harriet that she was a Nervous Nellie. The couple had six children: two boys, Alfred and Henry Jr., and four girls, Luella, Catherine, Elizabeth and Beatrice. Harriet ran a loving, welcoming household. As there were no schools nearby, she brought in a governess to teach the children.

Talbot's calm, steady ways soon saw him appointed as magistrate for the area. Mr. Dyer, a devoted grandfather, never fully recovered from the overland journey and the hard work in the mine, and passed away in 1875.

That same year, Joe and Henry Morgan came to stay with William and George Palmer, as the mine was no longer producing. Within a year Joe, acting on a "gut feeling," asked for and received the hand of the Talbots' governess. The couple settled nearby, began ranching, and planted an orchard.

Luella had returned to Victoria in 1865 to attend school at St. Ann's Academy. Upon completion, she became employed as a governess in Victoria, and met and married a doctor visiting from England. The couple departed for England shortly after they were married, to take up residence there. Luella and Harriet corresponded regularly, but never saw each other again.

William never married, and took over the family ranch after Mr. Palmer died in 1880. Henry Morgan eventually returned east to London.

Harriet's famed stubbornness and determination helped to rebuild the family's lives when their home, possessions and store were burned in a devastating fire in 1885. A year later, she again had to summon up all her strength when her daughter, Beatrice, drowned. Beatrice was buried in the family plot next to her two grandfathers.

Despite her busy life with the ranch, the store and raising her children, Harriet could often be found sitting on the shores of the lake, painting or sketching the hills surrounding her. Her eldest son, Alfred, inherited and surpassed Harriet's skill, and went on to study art in England and France.

When Harriet turned fifty she took her money from the mine, which she had saved in the bank, and she and Talbot went on her long-desired trip to New York. She recorded her journey there in another diary, though this one was leather-bound and did not contain accounting columns. While in New York she thought often of Old Jackson, but she never saw or heard of him again after he said goodbye in 1862.

In 1902 Harriet died of cancer at the age of fifty-three. Talbot died a few months after her, of heart failure. Harriet's diary of her overland journey remained in the family, a cherished possession that was passed down from daughter to daughter.

Historical Note

Gold! In 1858, rumours of a gold discovery on the Fraser River in British Columbia raced around the world, enticing shop clerks, farmers, merchants, teachers, lawyers and doctors to leave home and family to seek their fortune. Thousands of men crowded onto steamboats in San Francisco to make their way north to Fort Victoria. Others spent up to five months on an ocean voyage from Europe and England, either going all the way around the southern tip of South America or taking the quicker route across Panama, and then sailing northward up the west coast to reach British Columbia.

More fortune seekers travelled overland from eastern Canada by stagecoach and steamship to the Red River Settlement and Fort Garry (present-day Winnipeg.) From there, in 1862, many would-be miners set off on a dangerous and difficult journey by cart, horse and on foot over prairies, rivers and mountains to the Cariboo gold fields. These adventurers were called Overlanders. Like all the travellers heading to the Cariboo, they outfitted themselves with tents, blankets, shovels, axes, picks, small stoves, cooking utensils, soap, needles and thread, boots, flannel shirts, firearms, candles and food: beans, bacon, flour, sugar, coffee.

The largest party of Overlanders, about one hundred and fifty people who set off from Fort Garry led by Thomas McMicking, included the Schubert family. Catherine Schubert was expecting her fourth child when her husband, Augustus, decided to leave the Red River Settlement to seek gold in the Cariboo. Determined not to be left behind, Catherine Schubert persuaded the Overlanders to let her and her three children join Augustus on the trek, not telling them she was expecting a child.

They left in early June of 1862 on a journey that was expected to take two months, but almost four months later they were still in the mountains of present-day British Columbia. It was a frightening, tiring journey. They forded rushing rivers, waded through waist-deep swamps, climbed steep mountainsides and cut their way through thick underbrush with axes. Mosquitoes drove people and animals nearly frantic, and wolves followed them, their howls shredding nerves already frayed by the constant fear of attack by Native people. Though the actual incidence of attacks was sporadic — at least for those travelling the northern route — any word of conflict, even between various tribes, stoked the Overlanders' fear. Strangely, other than at the various forts and missions, the McMicking Overlanders encountered few Native people until they reached Tête Jaune Cache, where they traded with a party of Shuswap.

Weary, some with bleeding gums and teeth loose from scurvy, and all with tattered clothes, the McMicking party finally arrived at the head of the Fraser River at Tête Jaune Cache at the end of August. It was decided here that they would split up. The Schuberts opted to take what they thought was the safer route down the Thompson River to Fort Kamloops, while others chose to raft and canoe down the treacherous Fraser River.

While floating on a raft down the Thompson River, Catherine Schubert was forced to stop at a Native village, and with the help of the women there she gave birth to a baby girl named Rose. The Schuberts continued on their journey downriver for three more weeks to Fort Kamloops and to the Cariboo gold fields, but had little success finding gold. Discouraged, they settled in British Columbia's Okanagan Valley.

The Fraser River party arrived at the mouth of the Quesnel in mid-September. Worn out from their journey and mourning the loss of some of their men on the river descent, all but a few of the Overlanders decided to continue downriver to spend the winter at Victoria or at New Westminster (at that time the capital of the colony of British Columbia). The next spring some returned to try their luck in the gold fields, while others started businesses or farmed or ranched, becoming some of the first white settlers of British Columbia.

In one of the parties was English artist William George Richardson Hind, who came from Toronto to join the Overlanders. He sketched and painted the trials of the treacherous journey across prairie, river and mountain, providing a rich legacy of Canadian history as valuable as gold. Bad-tempered at times, he was asked to leave one party of travellers and had to join another to continue his westward journey. His overland journey and Cariboo paintings and sketches were not discovered until 1927, when they were found in his brother's attic in Nova Scotia, providing all Canadians with a rich heritage. Hind's entire *Overlanders of '62 Sketchbook* can be viewed on the National Archives website.

Getting to the gold fields by any route involved a difficult water or land journey. Not only did the miners have to shoot rapids, but walk through swamps and fight their way through forests, often climbing over huge fallen trees. But the lure of gold and a chance to make a quick fortune was stronger than hardship or fear, and soon thirty thousand men swarmed over the Lower Fraser River, checking each gravel and sand bar for "colour." If they were successful, they staked their claim and got down to the serious work of mining.

Gold on the Fraser River was extracted by panning, rocking or sluicing. Panning was slow and not too effective, and was often used mainly for testing. A shovelful of dirt was placed in a pan. The pan was then dipped in water and moved in circles. Using his fingers, the miner threw out large stones and broke up the dirt to let it float out of the pan. The heavier gold remained on the bottom of the pan.

Rocking was a quicker way to find gold. The miner would build a "cradle," a wooden box set on rockers with small strips of wood nailed to the cradle's bottom to form ridges. He shovelled a small amount of dirt into the rocker, and added a bucket of water, while rocking the box. The lighter dirt and stones washed away, but the gold settled against the ridges. With one man to shovel in dirt and a second to rock the cradle, two hundred buckets a day could be checked for gold.

Sluicing required a steady supply of creek water. The sluice-box was a long wooden trough, again built with ridges or "riffles" on the bottom to catch the heavier gold. Dirt and gravel was shovelled in, and as creek water flowed down the length of the sluice, it washed away the dirt and stones, leaving the gold caught on the riffles. Many miners formed companies of six to twenty people to make it faster to extract the gold.

Along with the miners flocking to the gold fields were others who wanted to make their fortunes not from finding gold, but from the gold-seekers themselves. They opened tent boarding houses, stores, eating houses, saloons and gambling houses. Opportunists eager to part the miner from his fortune — pickpockets, thieves and gamblers — also flocked to the gold fields.

Alarmed by the sudden arrival of thousands of gold-seekers, James Douglas, the governor of Vancouver Island, extended his authority to cover the Fraser River area as a British holding. The British Parliament quickly formed a new colony that included the Fraser River and its tributaries from the Rocky Mountains west to the Pacific coast, south to the international boundary and north to the Peace River. It was named British Columbia by Queen Victoria. James Douglas was appointed governor of the new colony. One of his first acts was to require that everyone seeking gold purchase a mining licence for five dollars. Customs officers enforced the licences, and later on, gold commissioners set up offices to issue the mining licences. Money from the sale of licences went to help pay for the development of the new colony of British Columbia.

As the Fraser River's gravel bars were stripped of gold, miners travelled almost 650 kilometres further into the interior of British Columbia. Here in the Cariboo, a region east of the Fraser River and south of the Quesnel River, dozens of small tributaries flowed into the Fraser. Accidents, many of them fatal, were plentiful as men and pack mules journeyed to the Cariboo. They toppled over steep cliffs or drowned in the fast-flowing Fraser River. Many men turned back, but others, like Billy Barker and John Cameron, persevered and were rewarded with rich claims. As in any gold rush, some miners made nothing at all, while others pulled in $40.00 to $300.00 a day from their claims.

On the many creeks, men banded together in companies and began to sink deep shafts into the bedrock and tunnel into the sides of the hills to find the elusive gold. The area was stripped of trees as wood was needed to shore up crumbling shaft walls against cave-ins, for cabins and shelters, for fuel, for windlasses (used to raise buckets of rock and dirt from the shafts), for sluices, and for the huge Cornish wheels (large water-driven wooden wheels used to pump water out of the shafts so miners could dig deeper).

As before, traders and business people followed the miners, and camps sprang up along the creeks seemingly overnight. Antler, Richfield and Barkerville were thriving places with stores, restaurants, boarding houses and churches. And because the miners needed entertainment, there were many saloons. Here the men played cards, ate meals and danced — often with each other, as few women lived in the settlements. But as the miners went on to other areas, one by one the settlements were abandoned and today those that remain are ghost towns.

Recognizing the need for a road into the Cariboo over which to pack supplies, Governor Douglas ordered the Royal Engineers to begin the Cariboo Wagon Road. It stretched 650 kilometres from Yale in the south to Barkerville in the north. The final section was completed in 1865 and helped to open up the interior of British Columbia.

To keep law and order in the area, Judge Matthew Baillie Begbie arrived from England. Judge Begbie had graduated in law from Cambridge University, and was a man well travelled and fond of adventure. He made the journey to the Cariboo to administer the law, and while there he mapped the area and recorded the weather and types of flora. He was regarded as a fair judge, not discriminating by race. Judge Begbie's nickname, "the hanging judge," came about after his death, and is considered part myth. His reputation of acting swiftly — and at times, harshly — along with the presence of a detachment of soldiers and police officers, helped to keep the miners under control. But the Cariboo was a large area of wilderness, and despite the presence of the law, there were still some cases of miners being robbed of their gold, or even murdered for it.

By 1864, one hundred companies had staked out more than three thousand claims along the Cariboo's creeks. While most of the gold was extracted by 1870, some claims were still being worked in the early 1900s. It is estimated that 30 million dollars' worth of gold was taken from the area. But more important than gold, a new province called British Columbia had been born.

Historical fiction is a mixture of fact and imagination. The overland journey and the Cariboo gold rush are fact. So are these people: Thomas McMicking, the Schubert family (Augustus, Catherine, and their three children, Gus Jr., Mary Jane and James), William George Richardson Hind, James Sellar, James Carpenter, Alexander Fortune, William Fortune, Eustache Pattison, James Wattie, William Wattie, Charles Rochette, Rev. Corbett, James Kelso, W. W. Morrow, Felix Munroe, Robert Warren, Alexander Robertson, J. Douglas, Dr. Edward Stevenson and Judge Matthew Baillie Begbie. The remaining characters in Harriet's story are from the author's imagination.

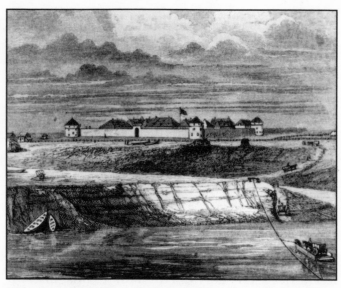

Fort Garry in 1860, including the ferry across the Red River (at lower right).

Thomas McMicking was selected by the other Overlanders to be the party's leader. He drowned four years after reaching British Columbia, trying to save his son William from drowning.

People departing Fort Garry in 1862. Artist William George Richardson Hind travelled with one of the parties, sketching people and scenes along the way.

Catherine Schubert, wife of Augustus Schubert, insisted on accompanying her husband. She was pregnant and gave birth to the fourth of her children at a Native village along the Thompson River.

A Red River cart train in 1862, pulled by horses rather than oxen.

The Overlanders had to cross many rivers. Sometimes the oxen and carts could be rafted across; other times the oxen were made to ford the river or even to swim to the opposite side.

A view that many of the Overlanders probably grew tired of, farther into the journey. The oxen were useful in crossing the prairie, and were used as pack animals once the carts were no longer practical.

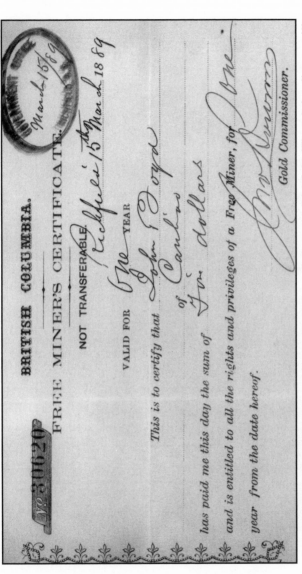

BRITISH COLUMBIA.

FREE MINER'S CERTIFICATE.

NOT TRANSFERABLE.

No. 30620

Richfield 15th March 1869

VALID FOR One YEAR

This is to certify that John Boyd

of Cariboo

has paid me this day the sum of five dollars

and is entitled to all the rights and privileges of a Free Miner, for One

year from the date hereof.

_____
Gold Commissioner.

An 1889 miner's certificate issued by the Gold Commissioner in Richfield. The mining licence still cost the same as in 1862 — five dollars.

153

A pack train of mules in 1868 Barkerville. Though mules were the most common animals used, oxen were also used with pack saddles.

One of the last camels used as a pack animal in the Cariboo. The animals originally came from Russia, for use in the California gold fields. Twenty-three were later brought north to British Columbia.

Native men and even women, like this group in Moricetown in the 1900s, were hired to pack supplies.

The Never-sweat Company tunnel, Williams Creek, 1868.

Men standing at the windlass at the Barker Claim on Williams Creek in 1867.

Prospectors panning for gold.

One of the huge Cornish wheels used to remove water from the shafts.

The Sheephead Mine on Williams Creek in 1867.

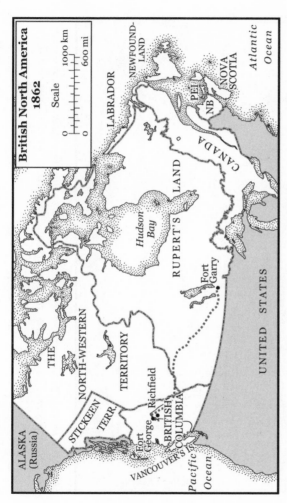

Canada in 1862, with the Overlanders' route from Fort Garry to the Cariboo.

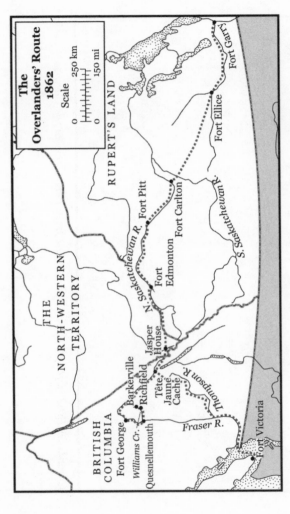

The Overlanders' main route to the Cariboo after crossing the mountains was down the Fraser River. The Schuberts and some others travelled down the Thompson River.

Acknowledgements

Cover portrait: Detail from *The Zandvoort Fishergirl, 1884* by Elizabeth Adela Stanhope Forbes, courtesy of Newlyn Orion Galleries Ltd., Penzance, Cornwall, UK / Bridgeman Art Library.

Cover background: Detail, colourized, from Mining Village (Richfield), Richfield, B.C., 1867-1868, National Archives of Canada, C-24290.

Page 148 (upper): Manton Marble, *Fort Garry in 1860*, Provincial Archives of Manitoba.

Page 148 (lower): Thomas McMicking, British Columbia Archives, A-01418.

Page 149 (upper): *Miners Leaving Fort Garry*, William Hind's *Overlanders of '62 Sketchbook*, National Archives of Canada, C-009583.

Page 149 (lower): Catherine, Mrs. Francis Augustus Schubert, British Columbia Archives, A-03081.

Page 150: William Hind, *Red River Cart Train*, Metro Toronto Library, John Ross Robertson Collection, T16352.

Page 151 (upper): *Crossing the Assiniboine from the East Side*, William Hind's *Overlanders of '62 Sketchbook*, National Archives of Canada, C-022710.

Page 151 (lower): *Ox cart crossing a river*, William Hind's *Overlanders of '62 Sketchbook*, National Archives of Canada, C-033708.

Page 152: *Rear View of a Harnessed Ox*, William Hind's *Overlanders of '62 Sketchbook*, National Archives of Canada, C-033710.

Page 153: John Boyd Miner's Certificate, British Columbia Archives, MS-2788 file 17.

Page 154: Pack Train, Barkerville, British Columbia Archives, C-08171.

Page 155: The Last of the Camels from the Cariboo Road, British Columbia Archives, A-00347.

Page 156: Moricetown, Indian Women Packers, British Columbia Archives, G-04121.

Page 157 (upper): The Never Sweat Company tunnel, Williams Creek, B.C., 1868, Frederick Dally, The National Archives of Canada, C-173.

Page 157 (lower): Windlass at the Barker Claim, Williams Creek, B.C., 1867-1868, Frederick Dally, National Archives of Canada, C-19424.

Page 158: Prospectors with gold pan, Glenbow Museum, NA-2426-10.

Page 159: Cornish wheel, British Columbia Archives, A-00558.

Page 160: The Sheephead, Williams Creek, British Columbia, 1867-1868, Frederick Dally, National Archives of Canada C-19423.

Sketches on pages 32, 63 and 102 by Bree Flowers.

Pages 161–162: Maps by Paul Heersink/Paperglyphs. Map data © 2002 Government of Canada with permission from Natural Resources Canada.

Thanks to Barbara Hehner for her careful checking of the manuscript; to Richard Thomas Wright, author of *Overlanders 1858 Gold*, to Dr. Jean Barman, Professor of Educational Studies at the University of British Columbia and author of *The West Beyond the West: A History of British Columbia*, and to Roderick J. Barman, Professor Emeritus of History at the University of British Columbia and author of "Packing in British Columbia," in *The Journal of Transport History* (September 2000), for sharing their historical expertise.

For my niece, Jennifer Haworth,
who has successfully scaled a few mountains herself.

About the Author

Barbara Haworth-Attard is hooked on writing historical fiction — many of her books are set in historical times. But her interest in the people who made the dangerous trek west to the Cariboo came about partly by accident. "It was when I was doing research for another book that I first came across the term 'The Overlanders,'" she says. "At that time I made note of the subject, as I often do when something interests me, and went on with my other book. So it was great to be able to go back and delve deeper into the Overlanders' amazing journey from Fort Garry to the Cariboo for this diary."

What drew her to the story was how the people — ordinary people for the most part, shop clerks and millers and merchants — managed to survive such a difficult expedition. "I am always intrigued by those people who are adventurers: those who look at mountains and want to climb, who look at oceans and want to cross, who look into space and want to reach stars. But even more fascinating are those people who perhaps are not adventurers in the true sense of the word but, like Harriet, are pulled into situations they might not normally find themselves in and, most importantly, rise to the occasion."

Harriet was a fun character to get to know, Barbara says. "One of the greatest challenges in writing historical fiction is to get the era in proper perspective with the character's eyes, and keep it true without letting the here and now creep in." For this she relies heavily on diaries and first-hand accounts to provide her with a window to the era she is writing about. "The most fascinating part of writing, for me, is creating a character who feels real by the end of the book."

Barbara admires Harriet's spunk and determination, something the people in the McMicking party needed to help them reach the Cariboo, as well. "For me, the story of the Overlanders is about inner strength; about going on when you do not think you can take another step, about eating skunk when you're hungry — and finding it tasty — and lending a hand to the person beside you who is stumbling. I look at Catherine Schubert, with three children and another on the way, climbing through swamps and forests and I think: I could never do that. But oddly enough, most of us could and would if we needed to.

"And thank goodness we do have daring and courage and perseverance inside, because these are the characteristics that settled Canada and will some day settle Mars, that produced vaccinations for smallpox and polio and will some day cure cancer; that produce music and art and even very practical things such as new farming practices." Barb likes to think that Harriet's story might encourage readers to go on towards their own dreams, even if they think they cannot take another step. Her advice (and Harriet's): "You really can."

Barbara has written more than ten books, half of them historical, the others fantasy and contemporary novels. She was nominated for the Governor-General's Award in 2003 for *Theories of Relativity*, the story of a boy who is struggling to survive on the street. Another novel, *Home Child*, depicts the life of a thirteen-year-old boy who, like many other "home children," is sent from poverty in England to the Canadian prairies as a labourer, and who earns the friendship of the young girl whose family took him in. *Home Child* was shortlisted for the Mr. Christie's Book Award, the Geoffrey Bilson Award for Historical Fiction for Young People, the Silver Birch Award and the Red Cedar Award. *Love-Lies-Bleeding*, a Geoffrey Bilson and Red Cedar nominee, is a World War I story based on Barbara's father's letters home from the war. *Irish Chain* is set around the time of the 1917 Halifax Explosion.

Copyright © 2004 by Barbara Haworth-Attard.

All rights reserved. Published by Scholastic Canada Ltd.
SCHOLASTIC and DEAR CANADA and logos are trademarks
and/or registered trademarks of Scholastic Inc.

National Library of Canada Cataloguing in Publication

Haworth-Attard, Barbara, 1953-
A trail of broken dreams : the gold rush diary of Harriet
Palmer / Barbara Haworth-Attard.

(Dear Canada)
ISBN 0-439-97405-4

1. Overland journeys to the Pacific–Juvenile fiction. 2. Cariboo (B.C. :
Regional district)–Gold discoveries–Juvenile fiction.
I. Title. II. Series.

PS8565.A865T73 2004   jC813'.54   C2004-900876-5

No part of this publication may be reproduced or stored in a retrieval
system, or transmitted in any form or by any means, electronic,
mechanical, recording, or otherwise, without written permission of the
publisher, Scholastic Canada Ltd., 175 Hillmount Road, Markham, Ontario
L6C 1Z7, Canada. In the case of photocopying or other
reprographic copying, a licence must be obtained from Access Copyright
(Canadian Copyright Licensing Agency), 1 Yonge Street, Suite 1900,
Toronto, Ontario M5E 1E5 (1-800-893-5777).

6 5 4 3 2 1   Printed in Canada   04 05 06 07 08

The display type was set in Stagecoach.
The text was set in ACaslon Regular.

Printed in Canada
First printing June 2004

Dear Canada

Other books in the series:

Whispers of War
The War of 1812 Diary of Susanna Merritt
by Kit Pearson

Alone in an Untamed Land
The Filles du Roi *Diary of Hélène St.-Onge*
by Maxine Trottier

Brothers Far from Home
The World War I Diary of Eliza Bates
by Jean Little

An Ocean Apart
The Gold Mountain Diary of Chin Mei-ling
by Gillian Chan

Banished from Our Home
The Acadian Diary of Angélique Richard
by Sharon Stewart